THE TIME EATER

By

Aaron J. French

JournalStone

JOURNALSTONE
YOUR LINK TO ARTISTIC TALENT

JournalStone books may be ordered through booksellers or by contacting:

JournalStone

www.journalstone.com

ISBN: 978-1-945373-36-7   (sc)
ISBN: 978-1-945373-37-4   (ebook)

JournalStone rev. date: January 27, 2017

Library of Congress Control Number: 2016962438

Printed in the United States of America

Cover Art & Design: 99designs - Hortastar

The Time Eater

"Now you must only dare to be tragic human beings, for you will be released and redeemed."

—Friedrich Nietzsche

"The tremendous world I have in my head. But how free myself and free it without being torn to pieces. And a thousand times rather be torn to pieces than retain it in me or bury it. That, indeed, is why I am here, that is quite clear to me."

—Franz Kafka

Chapter One

What can you see looking through a half-full glass of whiskey? A scrawny orange-and-white alley cat trying to scratch his way through the window. Why the hell would he want to get in? There's nothing here for him. There's nothing here for anyone.

At that moment, the smartphone rang. A husky but intriguing voice said, "You don't know me. My name is Annabelle. James Steiner is dying. You've got to meet me at Grand Central Terminal. Bring a suitcase."

I was long past caring what happened to me. What the hell? Why not? I packed my things and headed out.

I was jarred awake as the train pulled into the station. My heart sped up and I noticed my left hand was twitching. As I stepped onto the platform, trying to get my bearings, I saw a tall, slender woman standing beside the ticket machines. She had long black hair and the face of a watchful hawk, wearing a leather coat and stiletto heels. Sinister class. She was Carolyn Jones as Morticia Addams. I had no idea how she knew me, but she came right over as I exited the train.

"Roger Borough," she said.

"How'd you know?"

She shrugged. "James showed me pictures of you at Ohio State."

Annabelle took my hand, clasping it in her own. A brazen act, which seemed to fit her character. A shiver passed through me. She had gorgeous eyes, big almond-shaped globes full of dazzling blue.

"Good thing you recognized me," I said. "I'd've wandered around this place like an idiot."

Instead of responding, she just stared at me. My hands and feet quivered with nerves and emotions. Finally she relented.

I appeased her with pleasantries and platitudes, though in my mind I was asking myself what I was doing here. I had given up on James Steiner long ago. Prolonged isolation and creeping madness made a person do strange things. Perhaps I'd known this day would come.

We took a taxi to her car, then she drove us through the city in her silver Toyota Camry, leather seats and tinted windows, footwells and a backseat exploding with Starbucks containers, food wrappers; buildings, cars, and people flashed by in the glass.

I don't need to see James.

I don't.

We headed in the direction of the Queens Midtown Tunnel, and I suspected we were on our way to Brooklyn. Why she hadn't asked me to drive there myself from Oyster Bay, avoiding the trip to the city, I had no idea. Probably felt this would be easier, or maybe she wanted to scope me out before bringing me to her home. I asked her about James to break the ice, hoping to convince her I wasn't crazy.

She said, "He wants to end his life as he began it."

"Which means?"

Annabelle shrugged. "I think he wants people around who care about him."

Doubtful. I knew what James fucking wanted, the son of a bitch. He wanted to talk about what happened that night.

He and I began this ignoring-each-other game immediately after college when James married Celeste Roughen, the artsy stuck-up, party-and-painting darling, poster-girl for some HBO mini-series. I married the psychotherapist Jenny Morgan.

I could never stand Celeste. I thought James married her because of what we experienced, like it had influenced his decision. After that night he'd wanted flowers, dancing, roses, weddings, traveling. He'd wanted nothing more to do with darkness.

Me, I was a glutton for the stuff, always had been. I got married to the dark.

We attended Ohio State together, graduated, and then went on our separate, married ways. James majored in business and, as far as I knew, became a hotshot corporate executive for some company that manufactured stereo equipment. I wound up teaching humanities at NYC Community College, basically a reform school disguised as an education institution. It was thankless work, but it kept me gainfully employed. Jenny and I bought the house in Massapequa straight out of college. After the divorce, we sold it and she moved away, while I clung to what sanity I had left and salvaged the apartment in Oyster Bay, riding the LIRR to my teaching job, reading obscure Edgar Allan Poe stories and fantasizing about draping my body across the tracks.

Neither of our marriages lasted long, though theirs had seemed lovey-dovey and successful. Mine was over in about five years—five steps into hell, with each year worse than the one before, and yet I couldn't leave. I was addicted, like an alky with the DTs. Five years trapped in a Dostoevsky novel, with Jenny playing Grand Inquisitor.

The experience was so nerve frying and traumatic that afterward I became isolated. I'd sworn off women completely and hadn't dated since, which basically served to disassociate me from the world. I'd tried repeatedly to change my attitude since the divorce, but I was living in a nightmare, the famous raven croaking "nevermore" inside my head. The whole period of my life post-Jenny had become surreal, dreamlike, viewed from the bottom of a whiskey bottle. That probably sounds hard to believe. I find it hard to believe myself sometimes. But that's the way it went down.

James's marriage lasted longer. Eight years. I heard about their divorce from a mutual friend, the kind of friend who sends you Christmas cards even when you've never returned the favor. This friend didn't know the cause of their separation, but mentioned offhandedly that the relationship had dissolved. I never found out why James and Celeste separated, and to the best of my knowledge, James never remarried.

Now this sudden request for contact, this terrible news that James is, what, dying?

What was I doing here?

He could be fucking this Annabelle woman.

Terrific.

I shook my head, trying to banish the thoughts, telling myself I was here because James was my friend, I cared about him, and that's what you did when friends got sick, you paid them a visit.

And yet... I'd always wondered, what would happen when one of us—James or I—died, now that we had seen what we'd seen, and done what we'd done? Would death bring an end? Or—and this made my skin crawl—did it officially *begin* with death? Could death be where the horror became real?

Annabelle pulled her Toyota onto the black asphalt drive, got out.

I'd been so lost in the ocean of my past that I hadn't noticed the confirmation of my suspicion. We were indeed in Brooklyn—the nice part of Brooklyn. Every house here looked the same: stately, two-story, redbrick, white trim, spotless. Flatbush Avenue ran before the houses, split down the center by a median resembling a small park. Benches and a walkway lined with grass, towering oaks.

"Nice place," I heard myself saying.

"I own it," she said, popping the trunk. "James moved in after he was diagnosed. At my request."

I reached in to collect my suitcase. "And the doctors are okay with that?"

"When the tests determined he had less than a month to live, they consented. That was three weeks ago. It's my wish for him to die peacefully in the company of his friends."

"A week? That's all he has left?" I was in shock. "What is his diagnosis?"

"Let's discuss that once you've seen him," she said. "I want you to take a good look at him first."

We headed up the stone walkway, pausing on the stoop as Annabelle searched for her key. There was a loud click as the door unlocked. She glanced at me, bumped the door open with a knee, and we went inside.

"I have a confession," she said, taking off her coat, gesturing for mine and hanging them both on a hook. I set my suitcase down by the door.

"A confession?"

"Follow me in here." We passed under a wooden arch to enter the living room. Most of the interior was redwood, covering the walls in heavy panels. The house gave the impression that it was very expensive. Maybe it was. Maybe she had money. The furnishings suggested as much: big leather sofas, oak bookcases with leather-bound books, stylish glass tables, a plasma screen TV.

"Do you like it?"

"Classy," I said.

She smiled. "Thanks. I try."

"You mentioned a confession?"

She paused a moment; then: "James didn't ask you to come. This was my idea."

The news hit me like a rib-punch. "What? He doesn't know?"

She shook her head.

The fear was getting real. It seeped into the walls, the furniture, reflecting in the glass front of the plasma TV, a yawning abyss. I thought of turning around, grabbing my coat, and marching the hell out of there. If James didn't want to see me, I sure as hell didn't want to see him.

But… he's *dying… don't forget that. He could die any day…*

"Are you angry?" she said. "Are you going to leave?"

I sighed. "No, I'm not going to leave."

"Oh good." She seemed to visibly relax.

"But what makes you think he'll see me? And what about his wife?" Now I had lots of questions.

"*Ex*-wife," she corrected.

I cleared my throat. "Yes, that's what I meant."

"That bitch Celeste will *not* be allowed near him. She's already getting his house. Don't ask me why he left that cunt's name in his will. My guess is that he forgot to take it out and now he's too far gone to care."

Her emotional outburst excited me. I found myself wanting her; strange to feel this, actually embarrassing. A long time had passed since I felt that way about any woman. Not since Jenny.

"Don't worry. James will see you," she said. "He *needs* to."

"Why's that?"

"Because he screams your name at night, a terrible scream that echoes through the house. At first, I would jump out of bed and rush into his room when it happened. He'd be sitting in there, covered in sweat and muttering your name over and over.

"But I've stopped going. It does no good. I only make myself more upset. Look. Whatever happened between you two, whatever caused you to stop being friends, James hasn't dealt with it. He hasn't resolved it. That's how I know he needs you."

She paused, then added: "What *did* happen, if you don't mind?"

"I do mind." That memory I kept locked away in the catacombs, and I wasn't about to let it out. "I'll see him," I said. "If that's what you want."

"And you'll stay a few nights?"

"But you don't even know me. Aren't you afraid?"

"I'm terrified," she said, "but of James, not of you. Please, I'm desperate."

I let out another sigh. "I'll stay," I said.

She straightened and came around the couch, came so close, and took my hand again.

"Thank you," she said, gazing into my face. "From the bottom of my heart I mean it, Roger. Thank you."

Forcing myself to look at her, I nodded.

She grinned reassuringly. "You seem very uncomfortable."

"I..." But I couldn't bring myself to finish the words. Mercifully, she let go of my hand and I was flooded with relief.

"He's up here," she said, heading for the stairs. "No sense delaying."

Chapter Two

The room upstairs was much darker than any sick room I could remember. Annabelle led through the gloom, stooping over the bed. There lay a thin, gaunt figure in the corner. Daylight was strangled by thick beige curtains.

"How yah feeling?" Annabelle asked.

A soft moan floated up from the bed.

Is that James? My god, this is what he's been reduced to, a thing tucked away in a dark room?

It was a sick guy lying in a bed. So what? Why did I want to get out of there so badly? After all, I felt sorry for him. Once, he'd been my best friend.

Annabelle came toward me, blue eyes glowing like sapphires.

"You can sit with him," she said. "I'll get dinner started."

"Couldn't we have some light?"

Her eyes flicked to the bed then back at me. She shook her head. "James prefers it this way."

"What for?"

Her face narrowed. "Because, Roger, he claims he doesn't wish to *see it*, anymore. Do you know what that means? What *it* is? I imagine you do. Perhaps you could talk to him about it."

She left us, closing the door, and a silence formed. That funereal light from the curtains made my head throb. I wanted desperately to let in some fresh air. Anything to rid the room of that faint smell of death, beneath which lurked another odor, reminiscent of sweat or urine.

I summoned my courage, crossed the carpet to the single chair by the bed, and sat down. The chair groaned beneath me.

I couldn't bring myself to look, so I surveyed the room. Shelves stacked with various books. A filing cabinet, half open, contents overflowing. Dirty clothes piles, appliance boxes, a collection of board games, even old cassettes.

"It's where you store things that you wanna forget about," James said from the bed. His voice was husky, weak, unnerving.

He continued. "You put things in here... well, because there's nowhere else to put them. They got to go somewhere, right? They once seemed so great, so important and useful, and so you can't bring yourself to throw them away. You just shove them in here, hoping they won't go away—hoping they won't *get* in the way."

I found the strength to face him. He was a silhouette in the dark. I noticed flashes of pale skin, nothing more. "Is that how you feel, James? Like you're forgotten?"

There was a long silence. Then he said, "Hello, Roger."

I released the breath held hostage in my chest. "Hello, James."

"Caught me at a bad time." He chuckled. "How the hell did you find me?"

"Your friend Annabelle."

"Friend..." He released a sigh that sounded like a dying wheeze. "Why'd you come?" He shifted in his blankets, propping himself up. I could make out a little more: shoulders, torso, arms. He was deathly thin, slouching with such dedication that, at a glance, he appeared insubstantial.

When he spoke, his outline shifted, rattled. "Why the fuck did you come here, Roger?"

I jumped. I was increasingly on edge around him. For one, we hadn't seen each other in a long time; two, he was terminally ill; and now: *anger.*

I don't care how long he has to live or how soon he'll be in the ground with rain falling on him...

...He's gonna talk first.

Despite the bravado, I said, "Same reason all these lights are turned out. Same reason you wake up screaming every night. Same reason Celeste left you—same goddamn reason Jenny left me—"

James sprang forward on the mattress, a shadow come to life.

The darkness grew arms, legs, and darted through the air, tackling me. I got a glimpse, just a snapshot of the thing he had become. The projecting jaw and nose, bony appendages, the contours of a rat. His eyes hollow, full of rage. I didn't know who the hell I was looking at, but my friend from college, this creature was not.

He landed on my lap without knocking me from my chair, chuckling as he leaned into me, applying the whole of his weight (which wasn't much). He felt like cardboard, stiff, like holding a corpse.

He pressed his scraggly face against me. His thick brown hair, cropped short back when I had known him, was now grown out, greasy, stringy.

"What do you know about my reasons?" he growled.

I met his sunken blue eyes. "Give it up, James, you know why I'm here. My life is hollow. I have to remember what happened, just like you. We can work together. It'll come back little by little, piece by piece—"

He spit into my face.

Wiping it away, I said, "You're upset because I mentioned Celeste."

He clambered off, back to his bed. I felt infected. I smelled his sweat, and my thighs burned from where he'd touched them.

Whatever he's got, I don't want it.

The door burst open and Annabelle appeared. "I heard noise, is everything okay?"

"Everything's fine," James told her. "Just two friends catching up." He grinned, his face like a rodent's.

She hesitated, gave me a look of suspicion, then went back into the hall, closing the door.

"You wanna talk about Celeste?" he snapped. "You think you know so goddamn much? It was your idea, remember? That night, I mean."

Before I could answer him, he said, "That night ruined me, man. Fucking ruined me." He laughed. "I have it figured out now. Some of it, anyway. You'd be surprised—hell, you'd be *proud*."

There was a long pause. I felt the room—the ceiling, the walls, the heaps of clothing—draw nearer to us. Dusk was fast approaching, seeping through the curtains, transforming the room into an eerie underwater dream.

"There is only the horror of that night," he said, "that thing in the sky... you remember, don't you, Roger? The way the sky opened up and all those—"

"—patterns and shapes," I finished.

His grin widened. "Now you're remembering."

His eyes suddenly shifted to the closet door by the bookcase. It was partially open.

"Go on," he said, "look in that closet. Celeste is *in there*." He paused. "Go on and see for yourself. She's fucking *in there*, man."

He's out of his damn mind, I thought, stunned. *It's fever sickness, dementia, all of the above.*

But I was already rising, moving through the gloom, moving on hollow legs up to the closet door.

"Open it!" he hissed.

I recoiled, shrinking into myself, but my left hand extended and closed around the cold bronze handle. I took a deep breath, turned. My fear blossomed. I felt tangles of arms spreading around my torso, down my legs, across my back. I was in total darkness. The room had ceased to exist.

My fear propelled me into the slightly darker notch where the closet had been.

It's exactly like that night! It's happening again. For God's sake, why? Why now?

I was remembering that which dwelled behind the flimsy veil of reality, watching, leering, waiting, the thing we'd summoned during the ritual years ago.

I groped the air, swimming in an ocean of ichor. The floor fell away and I floated on a wave of something etheric, halfway between delusion and lucidity.

My hands bumped against a cold, hollow object, like an empty tree trunk or a vacated insect carapace. I took hold, squeezed it, but could not see. Not until a fanning ray of light came dancing out of the dark, illuminating the closet, the claustrophobically close walls, and the corpse, that which could not, should not, be there, but *was* there.

Celeste slumped in the corner, head down, eyes closed, her hair tangled. Her body appeared deflated, the skin soft and wrinkly. For a moment I was transported to the past, recalling what it was like to be sitting in class with her, to resent her. How I would feel whenever she talked about James, how I came under the impression she was stealing him away from me, that it was her fault our friendship had dissolved.

She's dead. James killed her.

Suddenly the soft wrinkly corpse lurched and flung itself off the wall. I screamed, then screamed again, retreating a couple of steps. Celeste lifted her head, opened her eyes and yes, they were as I remembered—hazel-colored, angled slightly down so she resembled a Siamese cat. Her mouth popped open and what I saw in there behind the gums and rotting teeth was madness.

It was inside of her. The thing from the sky, the thing from that night.

The Time Eater…

The trio of words knocked the breath from me. Peering into Celeste's mouth was like peering up at the sky when it opened that night. I saw stars, planets, comets, suns, rolling and diving aimlessly. That incomprehensible thing dwelling *behind* the universe, sucking planets and stars into its gigantic black hole.

The vision seemed to pulse as the maddening image poured out of Celeste's rotting mouth, and then she was on her feet, thump-thumping across the carpet, arms raised.

I stumbled back, knocking against the closet door. The vision spilling from her mouth burned my retinas and I went partially blind. I retained enough sense, enough coordination, to thrust my balled fist into the dead woman's chest, sending her back toward the closet's rear wall. I curled my fingers around the edge of the door, hurtling it closed.

James's spectral laughter invaded my ears. Celeste rejected her imprisonment, beating ferociously at the door, and I was forced to apply all my weight to keep her from escaping.

Then a harsh glaring light spilled into the room. James's laughter was cut off mid-trill as he plopped onto the bed. The violence behind the closet door ceased.

Cautiously I stepped away, wondering if there had ever been someone banging on it.

"What the hell's going on?" Annabelle asked.

Chapter Three

We were downstairs in the kitchen, the two of us, eating a dinner of carrots, beef roast, and peas. We drank ginger ale. Her kitchen, like the rest of her house, exuded good taste. Oak cabinets, purple and black marble countertops, a stainless steel sink with double basins; a window over the sink, partly concealed by reddish curtains, enabled the night to enter the room.

"He isn't well," she said. "He's sick and it's getting to him mentally."

"Will you tell me his diagnosis?"

"It's a brain tumor. The doctors don't feel confident a surgeon can reach it."

I cringed.

She glanced at the ceiling. "Sometimes I think I hear noises coming from his room. But then I check on him and he's fast asleep." She looked back at me, forking a carrot into her mouth. "Never had it happen while company was over."

I gave a brisk nod, mostly a formality, but also a behavioral pattern I picked up during my marriage with Jenny. Jenny had demanded I respond to everything she said, no matter how arbitrary. I'd gotten in the habit of nodding whenever she spoke to avoid a shouting match.

And now you're doing it with Annabelle.

Shut up.

Jenny also got me in the habit of analyzing everything psychologically, drawing clinical conclusions from body language, behavior, and actions, connecting the dots and reacting accordingly. We spent so much time together talking about it that I'd eventually picked up some of what she did for a living. It was both a blessing and a curse. I didn't necessarily *want* to psychoanalyze interactions with Annabelle at this point... but I couldn't help it.

My thoughts wandered from Jenny to James, to the upstairs bedroom, and Celeste in the closet. Had I imagined it? No, Annabelle heard the banging too. Yet it had stopped the moment she opened the door.

We finished our meal in silence. I sipped the ginger ale to clear my head.

"You talked to him?" she asked.

"We talked."

She emptied her glass in a single gulp, stood from the table, and went to put her dishes in the sink. She kept her back to me, rinsing a plate. She wore tight blue jeans and I found myself staring at her ass.

What's wrong with you, I thought, catching myself. *You remember what happened with Jenny? You haven't dealt with that wound yet and here you are eager to carve another one.*

I'm not eager, I told myself. *Believe me.*

I found myself carrying the plate over and placing it in the sink, standing very close to Annabelle, smelling the fragrance of whatever beauty products she used, the lilac and passion fruit in her hair.

I remembered *it* then. The thing behind the veil of reality that I first saw that night twenty years ago with James. The thing in Celeste's cadaverous mouth, sucking everything into its vast black hole—planets, stars, meteors, quasars—the Time Eater, consuming time itself, consuming everything...

I noticed Annabelle crying. Water was washing over the plate and down the drain, but she had stopped moving.

I turned the water off, placing my hand on her shoulder. The instant I did, it was like another shockwave passed through us. I almost jumped from the intensity.

"Sometimes I think *I'm* the one who's crazy," she said, sobbing. "You don't know what it's like being here with him. I thought it would be a good thing, you know?"

Her eyes narrowed. She displayed that hawk's sharpness. "It's not pleasant, not at all. James has gone mad—or I have—but either way the things happening around here are crazy. I can't stand it."

She looked at me, and when she did I almost cried myself, even though I had no reason to. "It's why I brought you here," she said. "If you must know, that's why. It's all linked to you for some reason. And now you're going to help me figure this out."

I started to speak, but she brushed past me across the kitchen, stopping under the archway leading to the living room. "There's a spare room across from James's. The bed has fresh sheets and there's a bathroom in there. My bedroom is at the end of the hall. Good night, Roger. See you in the morning."

I stood alone in the kitchen under the feebly glowing lights.

* * *

Green, glimmering grass, the sun high overhead. Surrounded by the looming library building with its Classical architecture, the redbrick hall with its antique clock tower, brick walkways, trees, lampposts, and a small brick circle with a statue of William Oxley Thompson in the center clutching a diploma—the end-goal of all the students on campus—dressed in his collegiate robes.

Jesus. Ohio State. Nothing's changed, it's exactly as I remember it.

I stood getting reacquainted as the sun began to move in an arc across the sky. So fast that a huge shadow passed along the grass, the courtyard, the buildings. I glanced up in time to see it vanish over the horizon. Then the world went dark. The campus lamps flickered on.

I saw myself. Not me now; me twenty years ago. A junior. There was James. Also young, standing next to me in the courtyard near the statue of the former president of Ohio State, the glare of the lamps silhouetting us against the brick and stone.

It took me a moment to understand that this was the night when everything began to fall apart, when James and I stopped being friends, when we decided to go our separate ways.

The night we experienced *it.*

I approached them and saw, yes, they had begun. The younger me was opening the blasphemous book, the large leather tome with brass clasps and a symbol on the front. Seeing it reminded me of the bookshop I had frequented, all my lonely hours in the library, my incessant occult investigations searching for the information to satisfy my soul—eventually coming here, to this book, this night, and this heinous ritual we performed. *The summoning of the Time Eater.*

They had drawn the red circle on the bricks at their feet, the two college kids who looked just about as scared as anyone. They stepped inside it, held hands and closed their eyes. The younger me started reciting from the book.

I watched.

The air became gossamer, revealing holes that were all around, turning the night into cheesecloth. The lamplight shone through these holes, illuminating the horrid black thing on the other side, something that slept, waited, contemplated—*dreamed.*

Even in my incorporeal state, I could hardly grasp the idea of that entity. It defied all my powers of perception and intellect. Seeing it wiped reality away, for somehow the thing was able to expose the illusion of physical matter, like some horrid, undeniable truth from which there was no escape—

—*that all was a dream.*

The world fell away, dropping like shelves of snow during an avalanche. It was as if a great wind had blown apart an arrangement of stacked playing cards. The buildings reeled back into the void, the grass uprooted and fired through the air like green bullets, the trees melted as if by intense heat, folding in on themselves and vanishing. The lamps bent inward, toppling over in consecutive order, spiraling up and pinwheeling away.

Reality shook, swayed, pitched, the holes growing, bleeding into one another, until there was nothing *but holes,* a swimming wave of evaporation. This wave swept all physical matter into its gulf.

The only remaining solidity was the piece of brick walkway enclosed within the red circle, on which the two college students stood, their eyes shut tight, their hands clasped together as they held on for dear life.

The shapeless form shifted behind the veil. Stars and planets twinkled in the darkness, infinitely stretching wide, and soon they began to *glide* toward the entity, as if sucked inward by its vacuum.

The Time Eater…

* * *

I awoke to a bloodcurdling scream I thought was my own. I was gasping and covered in sweat, sitting upright in a foreign bed, in a foreign room, tangled up in strange bed sheets. The window at the opposite end was flung wide, letting darkness and a high wind into the room. The shutters beat against the outside of the house. I could hear the sound of traffic, and some asshole shouting at the top of his lungs—

—and that scream. It echoed through the materials from which the house was built. I closed my mouth, hoping to silence it, but it went on and on. I soon realized it was coming from *inside* the house.

From James's bedroom.

* * *

When it finally stopped I waited to see if Annabelle would assist, but I heard nothing. I remembered her saying she'd stopped going to him whenever he screamed. That it only made her more upset.

I got up to close the window, then reclined in the bed and stared at the ceiling for a long time. Once or twice I thought I saw the wooden beams melt away. There was daylight before I managed to fall asleep again.

* * *

I stumbled into the bathroom sometime the next morning. It felt like I had slept for hours, but the clock on the wall said it was only 9:30. I unpacked my toiletries and went to work, taking a nice hot shower. I dressed and headed toward the stairs, casting a sidelong glance at the closed door of James's room.

The house seemed deserted. I couldn't find Annabelle, but there was a glass of orange juice and a plate of eggs on the kitchen table. I ate the meal in silence, my mind running through the events of the previous day.

While I was washing my glass and plate, I heard the front door open and close. I turned and there she was, entering the kitchen. She looked as gorgeous as ever, having applied her makeup to perfection. Her face resembled a Grecian sculpture, but a furrowed brow belied her soft appearance.

"Morning," I said.

She glanced at her wristwatch. "Almost noon. Did you sleep?"

I nodded… then shook my head.

"The screaming?"

I nodded again.

She came and joined me by the sink. "Happens almost every night. Any idea why?"

"Nightmares from his illness, maybe? Fear of death?" I met her gaze, hoping this would satisfy her, but she clearly wanted more. I was not up to the task of explaining it.

She went to the table and sat down. "The police called."

A knot formed in my stomach. I kept seeing Celeste's reanimated corpse slumped in the closet. Kept remembering the way everything had *shifted*, shrank down, just like it had that night on the Ohio State campus.

"Oh?" I said, taking the chair across from her.

She knows, she knows, she knows—

"Celeste is missing."

The knot tightened. "Missing?"

A flicker of suspicion passed in Annabelle's eyes. "Yes, missing," she said, her voice adamant.

"How can she be missing? You said she was getting half of James's estate. And where were you this morning? I woke up and the house was deserted."

She squinted slyly. "I left you breakfast."

I smiled. "That's right, thank you. I don't mean to be rude. I was frightened when I woke up. James sounded like he was being murdered last night. I almost went to him."

"Good thing you didn't. There's no talking to him when he's like that."

"Tell me about Celeste."

She sighed. "The policewoman called here early, around 7:30. Said she wanted to ask James some questions about his ex-wife's disappearance. She'd already spoken to the hospital and they told her where he was. I said I had no idea what she was talking about. But she wanted to know if he's responsive. And so I lied. I told her that he seldom spoke now and when he did it was gibberish. Then she asked about me. If I was able to come to the station and answer some questions. After I finished feeding James breakfast, I went."

"What did they want to know?"

"The usual. Last time I'd seen Celeste. Last time James had seen her. If she had tried to contact either of us."

"What'd you say?"

"I told the truth. I said I hadn't spoken to the bitch. As for James, he wouldn't even know if he was in the same room with her."

That isn't true and you know it. Was she covering for him? I didn't want to believe Celeste was missing. If I did it meant that what I had seen the day before was real.

"What else?" I asked.

"They were reluctant about divulging details to me, but I was insistent and managed to get some information. She's been missing a week. The last time she was seen was leaving her health club late last Saturday. She'd been doing laps in the pool. The kid at the front desk claims she was perfectly all right when she left."

"Has she remarried? Does she have kids?"

"She's got kids, yes, two of them. But they're not actually hers. Stepchildren. She married a doctor several years after the divorce. Kids came from a previous marriage. They're also divorced, so she probably lives alone, I'd imagine. But I believe she stays in contact with the step-kids."

I recreated my memories of a young Celeste. Sometimes the three of us—Celeste, James, and I—would have lunch in the food court together, but that hadn't lasted long. Her face already began fading from my mind by the time I left college, like the memory of a dream—her name and presence there, but her face obscure. Once she and James started palling around, he dove into her completely, seeking refuge from the ritual, the Time Eater, me and my occult activities, and all the rest. The happy couple departed Ohio State with degrees in hand and faded from my life like an old Polaroid.

Fast forward to last night, the horrible abomination in James's closet. That wasn't Celeste, couldn't be. That was… what the hell was that?

The Time Eater. The thing James and I summoned twenty years ago. It has her now. It sucked her into its orbit, like all those planets and stars and quasars and—

"Do you suspect foul play?" I asked.

She locked eyes with me. "I don't know. I'm too tired to think about it. I'm stressed enough as it is. And I have work deadlines approaching."

"I've been meaning to ask what you do for a living."

"Freelance writing and newsletter writing. I do a lot of website design and editing, too."

"Do you write fiction?"

"All over the map. At the moment I'm working on developing a web-blog for a professional golfing magazine."

"You know about golfing?"

"No, but all the information I need is at my fingertips." She typed on a phantom keyboard in the air.

I smiled. "I had the feeling it was something like that."

"How so?"

"The way you live, the way you've got your house set up... I don't know, but it suggests a cultured, self-sustaining person, as opposed to a nine-to-fiver."

She made a face; this managed to get a laugh out of her. "Cultured? If you say so. I always thought I lived like a bachelor."

This made me laugh. "There's truth to that!"

After an awkward silence, as though we'd run out of things to say, Annabelle got up, pushed in her chair, and headed for the hall.

"I'd better get to work," she said.

"What am I supposed to do?"

She reached into her coat, withdrew a set of keys, and tossed them on the table. They landed with a crash. "Take my car anywhere you like. You can also watch television in there." She pointed toward the living room. Her face became serious. "Maybe you'd like to spend the afternoon talking to James?"

Chapter Four

I didn't spend the afternoon talking to James. I spent it exploring the lesser-known regions of Brooklyn, the slummy to the sublime. Its boroughs and ethnic neighborhoods, its high-rise redbrick buildings, and all the little shops and eateries. It had that usual New York charm, as well as its usual grime.

When Annabelle left me sitting at the kitchen table, I experienced an existential crisis. I knew the best thing to do was go talk to James, but I was afraid. I didn't think my sanity could stand it. I'd gotten through the previous night by telling myself I'd imagined everything. But now Celeste was missing. I could no longer use that excuse.

I snatched her keys, grabbed my phone and wallet from upstairs, and headed out. But as I was leaving I bumped into an attractive African-American woman tromping up the stoop, dressed in blue hospital scrubs and carrying a black bag.

"Pardon me," I said.

She waved. "Nah, don't worry about it. My fault, my fault." She continued up the steps, opening Annabelle's front door.

"Where are you going?" I said.

She regarded me coolly. "I'm the nurse from Beth Israel. I come to check on my patient."

"Annabelle didn't tell me a nurse was coming."

The woman raised her eyebrows. "Well Annabelle didn't tell *me* some man was comin'." She did a little flick of her wrist and went inside. I crossed the driveway to Annabelle's Toyota, backed out and drove away.

The hours of aimless sightseeing ended, at some length, in a place called Canarsie, known for its pier. Something of a poorer district, crowded with low-income housing projects, parking lots, and big grassy plots. Black folks milled about everywhere, and I felt self-consciously

Caucasian. Men with dreadlocks and women in African floral dashikis moved along the sidewalks. When they spoke, I noted their Caribbean accents.

I parked the car at the pier and got out. A dilapidated boardwalk ran alongside the muddy Jamaica Bay. The place seemed deserted, with overgrown weeds clutching old papers and trash. I did see a person or two standing by the railing, looking across the water with fishing poles cast over the side, staring toward the Manhattan skyline.

I sat on a bench, enjoying the sound of the wind and the soft rumble of the water, distracting myself because I didn't want to face the facts. I'd come to believe that women had a peculiar way of etching themselves onto a man's existence. Once you let them in, there was no letting them out. I was bitter. After these women left you for some hot young social worker, maybe some ex-junkie punk; hell, some rock-climbing stud—they remained in your unconscious, swimming around like fish in an aquarium, until you had dreams about them, held imaginary one-sided conversations with them.

Jenny haunted me. My *mind* was what she haunted, not my physical body, not my apartment back on Long Island. My thoughts. Why had the experience been so horrible? Wasn't the first time I'd asked myself this question. If I had advice for the fledgling bachelor community, it would be "never get married to a psychologist." That's asking for a mindfuck.

Despite Jenny's expertise of the human condition, she couldn't save our marriage. Maybe she never tried to. But I couldn't bring myself to accept that. The most depressing idea I could think of was that she hated me so much she'd giddily let it all go up in flames. My greatest fear was that she'd engineered our relationship—the courtship, the marriage, the divorce—like some kind of science experiment. Paranoid? Perhaps.

She used to speak to me with such clarity and directness—such coldness—that her words burst in my unconscious like arrows through a straw bale. Even now, after fourteen years—which is a very long time— her words remained with me. She'd left a size-seven carbon footprint on my brain. It was all I could do to shut her out with bitterness, solitude, whiskey, and time.

Sitting by the weatherworn boardwalk, the crystal dark waters up ahead, the breeze on my face, my thinking became lucid. These were the moments where my perception of her shifted. Had she really been the kind of woman I remembered her to be? Or were the other memories I had—such as her and I going to the movies, having dinner together, making love on the sofa in the living room—were these the reality of my experience? How could I know the difference?

Suddenly, a little boy came running along the boardwalk in front of me, his feet thumping loudly on the wood planks. I leaned back on the bench as his mother, a young brunette in her early twenties—scarcely a child herself—hurried after him.

"Come back to Mommy," she called, catching up to the boy, then scooping him deftly into her arms. He struggled for a moment before she managed to subdue him.

"You have to stay with Mommy always," she scolded, with genuine concern in her voice. "Remember, I know what's best. I don't want you getting hurt."

The child, gazing over her shoulder at the water, nodded. "Yes, Mommy."

Setting the boy down, they continued walking along the boardwalk, holding hands.

I tried returning to my brooding, but the scene with the mother and son had triggered a memory of the vacation to China we'd taken a year or two into our marriage. We had already started fighting. Conversations turned into arguments far too often, and the only time we got along was if one of us made a conscious effort not to get upset. Jenny had a cousin living in China named Brad, a working economist who moved to Hong Kong after college and made a fortune in their free-trade system. None of the details of his work made any sense to me. It was all over my head.

Brad bankrolled our trip to China, and we stayed for a week and a half. The first few days were difficult, as Jenny and I remained in our normal routine of arguing and bickering. But by the third day we started getting along. After that it was smooth sailing, and we had a wonderful vacation.

The three of us went on a train ride through the Yellow Mountains. Brad had this idea that he would show us uncultured rejects what China was about. Real China, *ancient* China, he said. Not what the PRC had turned China into.

Our destination was Chongqing, where we'd view the magnificent Buddha statues carved into the cliffs. But first we made a stop in Fengdu, The City of Ghosts, a place of spirits, demons, and ancient customs that would soon die out. Fengdu, Brad said, was one of the towns that would be drowned in the Yangtze River when the PRC completed its massive dam project. He went on and on about the deficiencies of the new dam.

Fengdu was magic. I scarcely recall much else from the trip, to be honest. But the Ghost City never left me. It was unlike anything I'd ever seen. A huge necropolis set in the side of the shaggy green mountain, shaped in the outline of a person who appeared to be rising out of the earth. An atmosphere of death and the afterlife surrounded the place, although the people living there were quite friendly.

At one point I went off on my own and discovered a Taoist temple. I read the signs in English, learning it was the Temple of Hell, a seat of judgment where newly dead were judged and then consigned either to Heaven or Hell.

I made my way up stone steps, flanked on either side by grotesque demonic carvings. The statues made my skin crawl. They looked very old, with terrible grinning faces, and some were poised in pseudo-sexual positions, while others crushed the heads of the living and even ate newborn babies.

I made it through this gauntlet, into the temple proper, and stood before the massive statue of a wide-faced Chinese man. The sign proclaimed him as "judge of the soul unto Heaven or Hell."

I remained there for a long time. An eerie feeling came over me, and I recalled, for a moment, the thing in the sky that James and I had witnessed years earlier. I hardly thought of it anymore; most of my energy was geared toward repressing the experience. But it came back to me in the Temple of Hell, reminding me of the instability of reality, how nothing was as it seemed.

Jenny snuck up behind me, touching my back. I jumped.

"Jesus, what's your problem?" she said.

She wore a long beige coat, with belt flaps hanging at the sides, and a white blouse with ruffles. She was fond of wearing her blonde hair in a bun, as she did now, usually with a barrette or two. Her chin and cheeks were slender. She had a small pointy nose and cool blue eyes.

"You're scared," she said.

I nodded. The judge of Heaven and Hell looked down on us from his perch.

"Of ghosts?"

"Yes—ghosts, and these terrible demonic statues. Did you see the one over there with the twelve-inch penis?"

She chuckled. "Must've missed that one. How about him?" She gestured to the wide-faced Chinaman.

"That's the judge of Heaven and Hell. He decides which souls are damned, and which ones enter salvation."

"And how did *you* fare against the judgment?"

She was acting amiable, and so I wanted to get along too. But a trace of my accusatory bitterness crept in when I aimed my thumb down and said, "Damned for eternity."

She took my hands. "I know we fight a lot, Roger. I think that's part of being married. I mean, you don't know anything about relating to another person. How could you? You're damn near a baby yourself. But I don't fault you for that. Sometimes, I wish you were more open with me. I just wish... when you looked at me, you didn't see your deceased mother looking back. Perhaps that's asking too much."

I'd grown to despise whenever she spouted her psychology mumbo jumbo. At the beginning, I'd found it interesting—until the hundredth time it cut into my soul. She was always right, which was the worst part.

I'd taken enough psych courses in college to understand a portion of what she meant when she said, *I wish, when you looked at me, you didn't see your deceased mother looking back.* It was true about my mother, and it was true I probably hadn't processed the experience. But it was all so confusing. Sometimes, I wished we could have normal arguments, about normal issues, instead of heavy cerebral shit about repressed emotions.

"I feel overwhelmed," I said. "I wonder if I'm capable of being your husband at all. It doesn't help that you're so willful and intense."

"Why don't you stick to speaking about yourself?"

"All right. I like you, Jenny, and I'm trying to work out all my anger issues, but for now, let's just enjoy the rest of our vacation. What do you say?"

She sighed. "Yes, we are getting along. But I want you to keep your snide and bitter comments to yourself. I know you're upset, and I know how you feel, but you don't get to take it out on me. Understand?"

"I understand."

"Good. Then come here to Mommy. Mommy knows what's best."

I put my arms around her, and she leaned into my chest. I kissed the top of her head. Then she said something that has stuck with me ever since. She looked into my eyes and said, "You don't understand, Roger. You've never understood and you never will. That's the tragedy with you."

We returned from China the following week. In no time we were back to fighting, but in spite of the mounting tension I didn't forget the way we had enjoyed each other's company. I don't think Jenny forgot it, either. We couldn't recreate those conditions in our day-to-day lives, however, and so our marriage fell apart.

Spiriting back to the present, I studied a group of seagulls migrating across the sky, their mournful cries echoing off the nearby project buildings. I thought I was about done with the boardwalk, and with Canarsie Pier, so I got up and walked over to the car.

Driving away, I felt nostalgic and sad. I hated that notch on my timeline marked *marriage*, but I simultaneously grieved for it and wished it back. What did that mean?

It means you're afraid of women, that you hate your childhood, that you're a baby. It means you have no idea how to relate to another person.

It was dark when I arrived back at Annabelle's house. I had been gone all day. It occurred to me that she might have needed her car. I'd had my smartphone turned on, so she could've called me if she needed it. Still, I felt guilty for having it.

A front of storm clouds was rolling in, casting its purple glow along the streets and sidewalks. Annabelle's house was dark except for the light in James's upstairs window. For a second, I thought I saw his silhouette staring down at me, a crooked shadowy thing lurking behind the curtains. I strained my eyes to see, but there was no one there. I went inside as thunder rumbled.

* * *

Annabelle made dinner. I washed my hands in the bathroom, then helped her set the table. We sat down, but a weight hung over us, and so we talked little. She asked where I had been all day. I told her. I asked how her work had gone. She said fine. Otherwise we remained silent: thinking about Celeste; thinking about James.

I was also thinking about Jenny and part of me wanted to talk to Annabelle about it. I determined that might do more harm than good. God forbid I break down crying right at the table. I doubted she had much nurturing to give after all she'd given James.

I decided to ask about the nurse I'd bumped into that morning, instead.

"That's Norma," Annabelle replied. "Beth Israel Hospital released James to me on the condition that I allow them to provide nursing care."

"What does she do?"

Annabelle chuckled. "All the things I couldn't imagine doing myself. She bathes him, changes his sheets and pajamas, and gives him his morphine injections."

"He's on morphine?"

"It's, like, his favorite thing."

"What else?"

"She checks his vitals, and he's got his bathroom and his bedpan in there, but he doesn't always make it. Norma deals with that. She feeds him sometimes, too."

"And he lets her?" This was hard to believe. That dark, malformed creature passing for James up there would refuse, in my opinion, any amount of charity sent his way. He seemed content to gnaw on his own misery and waste away. I couldn't imagine him interacting with anyone aside from Annabelle or myself.

"Oh, he lets her. In fact, he has a crush on her."

"He was always popular with the ladies."

Suddenly she burst into tears. Her emotion startled me. There'd been no warning. She had cried a little the day before, but nothing compared to this. She was sobbing so hard her body shook.

I felt too stunned to move.

Why not comfort her? She's not Jenny.

Fuck it. I got out of my chair and stood behind her. She had her face in her hands, hiding like a frightened child, sort of curling in on herself. The arc of her spine protruded through her sweatshirt. I took a long deep breath and managed to put my ex-wife out of my mind, then placed my hands on her shoulders and started massaging.

She responded instantly, reaching up, pressing my hands tighter against her body. Her black mane spilled through my fingertips. She sobbed louder, but eventually started to quiet. I dug my thumbs into the spaces between her scapulae, moving them in circular motions.

How long has it been since someone's touched her? I wondered. And then, with my usual bitterness—*as long as it's been since someone's touched me.*

Jenny's voice popped into my head: *You have no idea how to relate to another person...*

It was true. I'd spent fourteen years of my life coming to terms with this, surrounding myself with friends and my students, the occasional "online chat-fling," but always failing to sustain something real, much less any kind of stable romantic relationship.

But oddly enough, as I stood behind this most beautiful woman and massaged her shoulders, I made the decision that I would get to know her, all of her, the real her. It happened just like that—like a flash of insight. I would figure out how I could relate to her as a human being. I wasn't going to be frightened, and I wasn't going to worry about getting hurt. I was going to be open.

She swooned to my touch, turning her head so her hair rested on my knuckles. It felt soft and smooth, like satin.

"That's nice," she said. "You're nice, Roger."

"I haven't always been nice," I said.

"Can't you take a compliment?"

Realizing that perhaps I couldn't, I said nothing.

"You're good at that. Had a lot of girlfriends?"

I laughed out loud. "No, I'm divorced."

She made a throaty grunt of comprehension. "Ah, I see. You haven't had *enough* girls, then?"

"Something like that."

"Well, I'm divorced."

"Really?"

"Three years now."

"How long did it last?"

"Length is not important. What's important is the loss of hope, the bitterness that takes root when relationships dissolve; that's the connection divorcees share."

"Wanna talk about it?"

She shrugged. "Okay, but there isn't much to tell. Jon and I met in the hospital where I used to work."

"You worked in a hospital?"

She nodded. "I wasn't always a shut-in, you know."

"What'd you do there?"

"Ran errands for doctors, did some filing and data entry, that sort of thing. Temp stuff. Anyway, while I was working there I met Jon. He was there part-time, until finally he established his own practice in Brooklyn, where I then decided to work. That's where we fell in love and decided to marry."

I stopped massaging. "Love, huh? Sorry, no such thing."

"It sounds silly, but at the time I do believe we were in love. We dated off and on for a year, then two, and we used to have such a blast around the office. God, I can still remember the practical jokes, the secret make-out sessions. We even had sex on the examination table a couple times."

"I always wondered if doctors did that."

"They do. We weren't the only ones doing it, either."

"Yeesh. Too much information. How old were you?"

She considered a moment. "About twenty-four."

This astonished me. "Wow, so you were married, what, ten years?"

"Eight. Seven if you disregard the year that we stopped sleeping together and fought constantly. Eventually he cheated on me and moved out. Left me the house. I've been here since."

"My marriage ended similarly. For a while it was like we were just roommates—ones that hated each other. Is that normal?"

"I think it is. I have a couple of girlfriends who stay married even though they're miserable. They're basically roommates who happen to sleep with each other after some drinks. Why they stay married, I don't know. Fear, I suppose. Being alone is scary."

I rubbed her shoulders another moment then started back to my seat, but she rose and placed her palms on my chest in a kind of *push*, gently sending me toward the countertop. She pursued, and when I was leaning against the counter, she pressed into me.

I could smell her luxurious hair, her skin, her makeup, even the lotion she used on her hands. *Intoxicating*. It had been so long since I'd held a woman.

"I'm lonely," she whispered, as if that explained everything; in a way, it did.

I held her closer. "So am I."

"Do you want to go upstairs?"

Panic shot through me. "Would we...?"

She slapped me playfully. "We're not going to sleep together, you jerk. Not yet, anyway. What do you take me for, a tramp?"

"No! I don't think you're a tramp. But I'm feeling a bit clumsy at the moment. I can't remember the last time I did this."

She chuckled. "At least you're honest."

She took my hand and led me upstairs.

This wasn't my reality. My reality was one of solitude, regularity, order. This kind of experience didn't happen. I imagined myself waking after a period of hibernation, like a bear emerging from its cave. It felt divine.

The hall was dark as we passed by James's bedroom. A dim light glowed under the door.

I pointed, whispering, "Is he awake?"

She nodded dismissively. "Norma cleaned and bathed him earlier, and I fed him dinner before you arrived. He likes to read at night. He's fine. Come on, you can talk to him later."

I assented, allowing myself to be guided down the hall. But at the last moment there came a sound, which I swore was *two* muffled voices, coming from James's room. I tried listening but it was gone instantly.

We entered her bedroom and she closed the door. For a moment we stood in total darkness. Out of nowhere, the image of Celeste—undead Celeste, the one from James's closet—popped into my head. I imagined her standing in the corner, that horrible mouth of hers yawning wide, waiting patiently for us to get into bed. Then she'd pounce on us, suck us into the cosmic void, the event horizon—

Annabelle switched on a little bedside lamp and the room flickered with light, and with relief I observed every corner was empty. Annabelle took my hand again, lying on the bedspread, drawing me down beside her. I was on my back, staring up at the knotted wood beams on the ceiling. Her scent was strong here. She curled into the crook of my arm, resting her head on my chest. I could hear the cycle of her breath. It seemed she had no lustful agenda, no ulterior motive. She sincerely did not want to have sex. She wanted to… *cuddle*.

I was relieved, as well as disappointed. I possessed the impulse to have sex, but who knew what problems that would stir up? The more I thought about it, the crazier it sounded.

I focused on the moment. Her body weight pressed against me. She felt soft and warm in my arms. Her scent, the gentle *whiss-whiss* of her breath. *Heaven*, I thought, closing my eyes. The words flowed through my head. I gave in to the exhaustion tailing me since my arrival.

I slept.

Chapter Five

Voices. Yes, voices. But not mine. Not Annabelle's. *James's voice.* And somebody else. Female. I listened closer. Familiar. *But where…?* Then I realized.

My blood went cold.

Annabelle had rolled off me during the night, so climbing out of bed unnoticed was easy.

I stood in the middle of her room, forgetting myself, forgetting where I was. Then I heard the voices again—James's and the other, the one I somehow recognized.

I left, heading down the hall, and paused before his door, palms sweating. Yellow light seeped out under the frame.

That can't be her, I thought. *Impossible. Even if it were possible, James wouldn't do that. He's my friend. Bringing her here would torture me.*

But I listened… and it sounded like her. There was no mistaking it.

That's fucking her!

I grasped the handle, thrusting the door open. Light blinded me, but I barreled into the room, driven by rage and contempt.

"Where is she?"

The violence in my voice surprised me. Realizing I could wake Annabelle if I wasn't careful, I lowered to a whisper. "I know she's here. I heard her fucking voice."

My eyes adjusted and the room became clear. I saw James sitting up in his bed, the sheets pulled about his shoulders, more sheets and blankets piled around him, so that he appeared to be encased in a kind of structure. The most unsettling thing was the way the mountain of bedclothes appeared to *move* occasionally, humping up and down, as if insects scuttled underneath.

He grinned at me, his face in shadows, his big eyes sagging. His hair stood out to all ends, giving him the appearance of being electrocuted. He looked thin and haggard, the remnants of a beard marring his cheeks.

I glanced to either side, searching. Gathering up my courage, I marched to the closet door, flung it open, and—

—jumped back at the sight of Celeste's decaying corpse slouched in the corner.

James tittered behind me.

He's lost his mind.

I wondered if I too had gone mad, for on closer inspection the closet revealed no Celeste, no withered corpse, no stars or yawning black infinities. I'd mistaken a pile of boxes and old clothing for a dead woman.

James roared with laughter. "You'll have a heart attack yet!" he blared.

I wheeled from the closet, anger boiling. "Where is she?"

"What's it to you? She's not your wife anymore. The matter no longer concerns you."

I watched as another sudden twitch ran through the pile of blankets, making them ripple. James was giving me that typical, unconcerned expression I remembered so well, but it occurred to me that he was only playacting, trying to divert my attention away from the movements in the sheets.

"Come on, you're crazy," he said. "Have a seat, let's talk. It's time we discussed this." He started coughing then, a deathly sound that wracked his frame and oozed phlegm.

My attention remained on the blankets. Great bulges rose and fell. One hump closer to James appeared in constant motion, bobbing with vigorous enthusiasm.

"What's that? What's going on there?" I demanded.

"It's nothing," he replied. But suddenly he threw his head back, arched up, and released a salacious moan that made my hair stand on end. His dark eyes went black and bulging, his mouth wide, tongue half out.

I couldn't stand this. It was making me ill. I had to know what was under the blankets. I rushed forward, grabbing the sheets in my hand, yanking them off the bed. They came away too easily, and I nearly lost my balance.

I stepped back, my jaw dropped. For the next few seconds I tried convincing myself that I was still asleep, dreaming, that eventually I'd awake and none of this would be real.

"*Jesus*," I heard myself whisper.

James tilted his head. He looked psychotic. His eyeballs jutted out of his skull. "Eh, what's that, Jesus you say?" He chuckled. "I hope this ain't a case of *no atheists in a foxhole*. I won't believe it. Not Roger Borough. Not—"

He broke off to release another morbid groan, and his thin body began to quiver. A line of drool graced his chin. I'd realized the cause of his orgasmic fluttering, and in horror my brain went numb, deactivated.

Jenny Morgan—my ex-wife, the woman I'd lived with for five years, had loved, yet still loved, but also hated—was lying on her stomach, her head in James's lap. Nude and young—not as old as she should be—her skin like I remembered: pale, milky, taut. Her blonde hair that reached almost to her lower back framed her head and spilled out across the mattress.

James was naked from the waist down. The sight of his wiry legs, boney knees, and sickly skin unnerved me. It was no mystery what Jenny was up to with the eager bobbing of her head. I felt nauseous, but I also felt myself getting aroused, which was terrible. I'd fallen asleep earlier with my clothes on, and so I bent forward slightly now, trying to conceal the front of my jeans.

"What's the matter, getting excited?" James crooked.

My eyes darted to him, my face flushing. "You *bastard*. What do you think you're doing? What the fuck is going on?"

He arched his body, and his eyes rolled into the back of his head. Paralyzed, I watched for several seconds as the act was completed. Then he pulled the sheet across his nakedness.

Jenny turned toward me. "Hey Roger," she said, smiling. "Long time no see. Have you been thinking about me?"

"He sure has," James said. "Bozo hasn't moved on a bit. He's even got my old childhood friend over here in bed, but all he can think about is Jenny, Jenny, Jenny."

I covered my ears. "Shut up! Shut up! *Shut up!*" I dropped down on my knees like a child.

Jenny's smile widened. "How good of you, dear. Just as Mommy would have it."

My skin broke out in goosebumps all over. I felt my entire world flying apart. She called herself that—Mommy—when she was feeling horny, or sated, or sentimental, or whatever. I'd found it disturbing then... but there were times I'd gotten into it.

She sat upright in the bed, golden-blonde hair spilling down her shoulders, her eyes piercing, her bare breasts exposed. She didn't appear the way she should; she was too youthful, like a woman in her early twenties, and her face shimmered with light.

She opened her arms to me, saying, "Come, my dear. Come to Mommy."

I fought the impulse to obey. "No! I don't believe you're real."

"Of course I'm real," she said. "Come over here. Find out how real I am."

"But... But I..." The words almost wouldn't come. All I felt was the delirium of my emotions. "...I just watched you giving head to my best friend! And now you expect me to forgive you? Fuck you!"

She giggled playfully. "You know that doesn't mean anything to me. Don't you miss me, honey? I miss you."

God, I did miss her. Every agonizing day for the last fourteen years, I had missed her. I could feel all the loneliness and frustration surging its way through my veins, animating me. I wanted to release it, once and for all. I wanted to be free.

"That's right," Jenny crooned, opening her arms wider. "Come and give your burdens to Mommy."

In spite of everything, I found myself rising to my feet, shuffling like a scolded child toward her. I didn't care anymore. I didn't care what she had done with James. I wanted to collapse into her arms, to let all my problems melt away, to finally die.

I'd barely reached the bed when James shot forward and shoved Jenny onto her side. It was such a violent act, unlike that of a mortally sick man, that it shocked me back to reality. Jenny pitched over to the right, her naked backside rearing up, and that—no, it couldn't be Jenny. No matter how much I wanted to believe, I just couldn't. The Jenny in my head, the one I thought about, despised, and yet longed for, the version of her forever preserved in her twenties—the version lying on the bed before me—that Jenny didn't exist. Not anymore.

All that existed was *it*... the thing behind the veil of reality.

The room darkened, grow smaller. The walls, floor, and ceiling disappeared, replaced by a depthless and black infinity extending everywhere. We floated in a bubble of dark air, somewhere in the outermost reaches of space. I could even see stars flickering and a few lonely planets.

James and my ex-wife now clung to the bed, as though to a raft, the mattress bucking and heaving beneath them. I could still hear James's horrible laughter. Jenny was prostrate, her arms spread to either side, clutching the box spring.

She screamed, "What is this? What's happening? Help me, Roger. Help me! Get me off this—"

I drew my limbs inward, curling my knees underneath my body and clutching at my chest. I tried to slow my heartbeat, focusing on my breath. I was invisible, not actually there.

The universe trembled. Stars shook, blackness quivered, planets rolled away, and James laughed his shrill, unsettling laugh, cutting through the air with his voice. I saw him on the bed, exposed from the waist down. He had climbed onto Jenny, was perching above her. He had his hands around her neck, throttling, bashing her forehead against the mattress.

"Help me, Roger, for God's sake! You're my husband and you're just sitting there like a baby! Mommy needs help—"

I put my fingers in my ears. Now there was muffled silence, like being inside an underground tunnel. I watched as the air started to distort, to resemble a stretched-out plastic bag. Stars began moving as if in a tractor beam, and the planets veered wildly off course. I saw a great blotch of stardust and space debris disperse into gigantic smoke clouds.

When I looked at James, my insides froze. The thing behind the veil of reality—the Time Eater—was pulsing through him, pouring out of him into the room. Suddenly I understood. *Oh my god, the thing has him. He's possessed!*

I shivered at the realization, as James's eyes went wide and black, like a demon's. His teeth poked out unnaturally from his mouth. His sickly skin appeared transparent and it had taken on a darker tinge, which I realized was the thing itself, shining out through his body.

A shadowy presence, perceptible in the scant starlight, moved above us like a giant storm cloud passing overhead. In the corner of my eye, I caught a glimpse: black, misshapen, blob-like. Stars and planets lodged within its massive form, assimilated by it, being *digested.*

The thing on the bed that used to be James threw back its head, baying at the sky like a dog, then suddenly this picture exploded into a thousand pieces, all dark and fluttering. Insects composed of the darkness itself swarmed around Jenny, dragging her into the swirling cosmic depths. She looked me in the eyes, extending her hand before vanishing into the churning black quicksand.

I lost touch with my body, my consciousness, and descended into a womb-like pit. In no time, I'd forgotten myself completely.

Chapter Six

When I snapped back to life, James was sitting upright, a shadow, a shade. Every patch of darkness in the room was accentuated by the yellow glare coming in through the curtains and spotlighting on the bed. I got up from the floor, my limbs aching, and felt a wave of nausea.

"Rough night?" James asked, not looking at me. His attention was trained on the battered old paperback he was reading.

I shook my head, as if to free it of dust. "What time is it?"

He remained quiet, then suddenly flung the book away in disgust. I picked it up and glanced at the cover. A collection of Edgar Allan Poe's poetry. I owned a copy of the exact same edition. Flipping open the pages, the book parted at a section that was heavily dog-eared. Without meaning to, I found myself reciting the verses:

> "It was many and many a year ago
> In a kingdom by the sea
> That a maiden there lived whom you may know
> By the name of Annabel Lee;
> And this maiden she lived with no other thought
> Than to love and be loved by me."

"I was never into poetry," James said. "I think it's dumb."

"Well, I happen to like it," I said.

"You would."

The silence grew longer between us and was interrupted only by a honking car or chirping bird from outside. I set the paperback down and dug in my heels, prepared to wait this out. Finally, James glanced at his alarm clock and said, "It's six-thirty. Early. Most of New York is asleep or heading to work."

I looked toward the door, and as if reading my mind, James added, "Annabelle should be getting up soon. She gives me my breakfast around seven-thirty or eight. Then Norma comes after that. I like Norma. You'll like her too. She reminds me of the girls we hung with at Ohio State. Smarter than shit, but not overly intellectual, and cute as a button. She gets me all clean, helps me onto the can—well, I can't be expected to make it there myself. Best of all, she brings a morphine shot. Mother's milk, baby."

I winced at the word *mother*, while another wave of nausea wracked my body.

"Are you in a lot of pain?" I asked him, changing the subject.

He became still. "You say that as though you wish it."

Maybe I do, you invalid son of a bitch.

"I am in a lot of pain," he said. "And I have to live with a perpetual migraine at this point. Some nights the pain is unbearable and I wake up screaming, yanking at my hair, battering my skull, thinking to myself *Get it out, get it out!* Have you ever had a headache like that, where it feels like a tiny rodent is trapped in your brain?"

His analogy struck me. Anger left my limbs in thick hot waves and I felt less irritable. *It's only James,* I thought. *A jerk, an asshole sometimes, but once my best friend. Now he's sick and dying in agonizing pain. I could show him some compassion.*

But I wondered, as I took the chair beside the bed, about the thing behind reality, if it had possessed James and taken him over. *Was* it still James? He seemed enough of his old self at the moment that I could suspend my disbelief. But this troubling idea lingered at the back of my mind.

The faint smell of death flowed from him. I imagined black wavy lines rising off his body, like the ones artists used to illustrate body odor in comic books.

"You look like shit," I said.

Darkness fled his face and he laughed. "I feel like shit. Don't let 'em tell you dying is easy. All that romance in movies about dying the hero's death, going out in a blaze of glory, that's all crap. Pissing yourself at two in the morning 'cause you can't make it to the bathroom, that's what dying is."

"Why can't you make it to the bathroom? You seem mobile."

"Sometimes I make it—most times, actually. Other times the pain is so severe that I get disoriented, or I'm too doped up to move, or my body's too fatigued. The closer it gets to the cutoff date, the less strength I have."

His eyes grew fierce. He leaned toward me, recapturing his old enthusiasm. "That's the worst part, you know? Turning into a baby again. Not being able to take care of myself. Feeling powerless wears me down. Honestly, I like Norma, I do. But sometimes when I'm leaning on her to get into the bathroom, and she's helping me into my pants, Christ I hate her more than anything."

"Jesus," I said. "Why?"

He shrugged. "It's like when you're a baby. You're in your crib wailing your guts out, then comes big towering Mamma to lift you up, comfort you, and make it all better. But you soon start to realize that you can't lift *yourself* out of the crib, can't make *yourself* all better. Then you start to hate Mamma. Why? Well, because she made you feel powerless. Not intentionally, wasn't her fault, it's just the way it is. This all occurs in the unconscious."

Something Jenny might say, I almost replied. That jolted me back to the events of the previous night: the terror, the strangeness, the morbid sex. *Enough of this small talk shit.* "Cut the crap, James," I said, "what the hell's going on? Have we both gone completely insane?"

The question startled him. But I knew—I absolutely knew—that he'd been sitting there waiting for me to ask it. He wanted to discuss this as much as I did. The only evidence I needed was right there in his eager eyes.

"There's a joy in madness that only madmen know," he replied. "This... *thing* that we drew attention to all those years ago, it exists in infinity, it feeds on time. The one true immortal, whose indifference is fierce, and, well..." He laughed sourly. "We had the stupid inclination to summon it out of its deathless sleep."

"It *was* a joint decision," I said, feeling the need to defend myself. "You stood inside that red circle same as me. Nobody twisted your arm."

He was silent; then: "Yes, I know. But let me speak frankly, Roger. It's hard not to blame you. After all, it was your obsession with... your *insane* attraction to the occult, those ridiculous books you picked up at yard sales, secondhand stores—"

"Give me a break, James, I was twenty years old. And I hadn't even gotten laid yet. What else can a kid in that position be expected to do? I hid from the world in my fantasies, so what? I can't remember much from those books now."

He guffawed. "Oh, you remember. You couldn't have forgotten the metaphysics section at the campus library. And what about Mitch Headrick, hmm? Forgotten about him?"

It felt as if a hand suddenly reached up and grasped my throat. "Mitch Headrick." I hadn't thought of that name in forever. Fragments started coming back. I knew I was disconnected from my feelings and emotions; I wasn't that ignorant, and besides, Jenny had pointed this out so often I eventually stopped trying to deny it.

But when James mentioned that name—Mitch Headrick—I realized that I truly was disconnected from my past. Instantly I saw images of the library, myself sitting at one of the empty tables, an array of books spread around me. I appeared frantic, my fingers agonizing over every page. I had a wild look in my eyes, as though I were peering into a magic crystal ball.

I recalled some of the obscure subjects: books on demonology, witchcraft, medieval grimoire magic, even ancient necromancy. I snuck away to the library every evening to read them, studying them with the enthusiasm of a monk transcribing the Gospels. I could recall moments when the librarians would come over and ask me to leave because the library was closing. I'd snap at them, tell them to leave me alone, to go fuck themselves, all sorts of colorful assholery.

"I remember..." I said.

"Keep going," he replied. "You'll get there. Listen to his name. *Mitch Headrick.*"

For some reason, that did it. As soon as he said the words again, a face popped into my mind: small, round, plump, pimply, and wearing thick glasses. The face had freckles and shaggy red hair and a large front tooth that jutted out past his upper lip.

Mitch Headrick—the local egghead, the campus doofus, the butt of so many jokes among the Greek life crowd. A smart kid. An honor student. Professors liked him, but his fellow students felt threatened by his intellect. And they detested his ungroomed, androgynous appearance. He got picked on, abused, harassed on a daily basis.

The most infamous Mitch Headrick abuse was the biology class pantsing. Mitch was giving his presentation in biology class on trophic levels and their impact on natural ecosystems, when Tom Simmons—a third-string receiver for the Ohio State Buckeyes—crept behind Mitch and yanked his pants down in front of the class, the professor, and two TAs.

The great humiliation wasn't so much the pantsing itself (under normal circumstances, the victim would pull their pants back up, hide their boxer shorts or tighty whities or whatever, and end of story). But for some reason Mitch hadn't worn any underwear to school that day. He later claimed it was because he hadn't done laundry in over a month.

The result was that the entire classroom was suddenly presented with Mitch's short, shriveled, uncircumcised penis. Even Tom Simmons looked surprised, crouching behind Mitch's kneecaps, a bare ass in his face.

The prank failed to yield the intended outburst of laughter; rather, there was an excruciating silence. Mitch threw down his notes, hiked up his jeans, and fled from the campus in tears. Tom Simmons was put on suspension the next day.

I remembered that Mitch used to hang around the library, same as me. His interests were math and science, whereas I orbited around the philosophy and religion sections. I never took much notice of him.

Then one day he sat down at my table, thumping a big black book about witchcraft down by my elbow.

Irritated, I tried to ignore him. When he wouldn't go away, I asked, "What's this?"

"You're that guy I always see reading books on the occult and metaphysics," he said. To my silence, he added: "I have a proposition for you."

As he spoke, I studied his appearance up close for the first time. He looked sad, and he had adopted that haughty intellectual air used by the downtrodden and bullied to make up for their feelings of inadequacy. I recognized it right away because, to some extent, I had done exactly the same thing.

"Could you help me with that?" he inquired.

I sat brooding, my wont in those days; if not in the library, in one of the campus's many bars, nursing a gin and soda with James by my side talking to some cute girl. James was always talking to cute girls. He had a way with women I could only dream after. I really only ever succeeded in picking up one girl. She, I decided to marry.

Mitch had been having trouble with a frat boy, a guy named Jerry or Jim, who was in the biochemistry class with him. Heaven knows what this frat boy was doing there. Mitch suspected he was there solely to torture him. Frat boys had stooped so low before.

Each day before class, this guy would corner Mitch in the lab and force him to hand over his notes. The guy barely ever went to class, and when he did go, it was only to space out or chat with female students. On the few occasions Mitch refused him, the exchange became violent and humiliating. He didn't beat Mitch, but he did something far more repulsive and twisted. He'd reach out and fondle Mitch's prick through his jeans. It was the lowest form of psychological abuse. The worst part was that Mitch had gotten aroused during these altercations.

Mitch was deeply distressed by the situation and seeking a way out. For some reason, Roger seemed like that way out.

Mitch wanted to stop the frat boy, but he also wanted to get even. I listened carefully to everything he said, for I could commiserate with his plight. I hated the frat boys, jocks, and campus rich-boy thugs, and I had experienced a few humiliations of my own on their account. So this idea of revenge I liked.

With our mutual interest in mind, we pored over Mitch's witchcraft book there in the library, with the afternoon sun streaming through the windows. I offered the extent of what I knew about metaphysics and the occult, and he put forward his entire knowledge of science, particularly geometry, and mathematics. The study of witchcraft was a rabbit's hole, so we tackled the subject as partners, developing something of a shared friendship based on our disdain for the world.

We met in the library every day and devised a method for revenge. It would be my first true magical operation. Mitch's, too. So we went to considerable trouble to ensure the safest accommodations. By the middle of the following week, the rites had been performed and I waited to hear back from Mitch on the results.

But I heard about it on the evening news, instead. Mitch was in the hospital, the frat kid too. Both had been assaulted by some unknown assailant. Police call-lines were open to anybody with information, as the report claimed neither Mitch nor the frat kid got a good look at the perpetrator, so there were no leads.

But I knew. I knew everything, sitting there in the dorm room watching the television and eating a pizza with James, who was my roommate. I acted dumb when James asked me about it.

Something had obviously gone wrong. Perhaps the frat guy had sensed trouble, called in a buddy for backup, and then a major fight had ensued. Or perhaps it was just some random act of violence, the kind the news reporters lived for. Or maybe... just maybe, the demon we had summoned that was supposed to attack only the frat guy decided to go after Mitch as well.

The incident was all over town for several days, but eventually it died down and everyone seemed to forget it. Mitch must have been totally freaked out, because he didn't return to school and I never spoke to him again. I heard he went back to live with his folks in Nebraska.

That incident was a turning point in my life. It forced me to come to terms with the fact that magic might actually work. All the stuff I'd been studying in those occult books clearly had some basis in universal truth, which hinted at a world beyond material existence.

"Good. Now you're remembering," James said.

I nodded, and as I did they all started coming back to me, all the people I had helped, all the ones for whom I had performed first white, then gray magic. People I read occult books to, talked with, counseled on their problems. People I interviewed and helped to devise solutions for their predicaments.

There were so many. I could hardly believe I had forgotten. A girl named Sally and her alcoholic boyfriend, to whom we had given a special herb to make him stop drinking. There was Marganita, the Peruvian girl, who had been raped by a boy named Teddy at a frat party; thanks to my magic, Teddy woke up one morning with genital herpes.

I remembered Kevin Bechar who wanted so desperately to pass his final exam in organic chemistry, but couldn't seem to retain the material; with him, we concocted a special meal made of certain etheric plant substances, which were transformed into knowledge about biochemistry.

I even assisted one of my professors: Dr. Reynold Mathews of the English department. It was his lovemaking prowess that needed help, given his age. I performed the ritual in his office and he reported back the following day, grinning ear-to-ear that it had worked.

"How could I forget?" I said, shaking my head in the darkness of James's room. "Did I find it all too traumatic? Did I block it out? Repress it? I mean, I always remembered I was into the occult during my youth, but I remembered it like a passing interest, a phase I'd grown out of. The rest of it... I totally forgot. Does that sound crazy?"

James chuckled. "No crazier than anyone. You know, it's funny. You used to be the authority on all this, the one who knew so much. Now the tables have turned, because I'm dying and that *thing* is inside of me. I have access to its consciousness. It has access to mine."

My hands clenched at my sides in the chair. "I knew it," I said. "I fucking *knew* that thing had a hold of you. What the hell does it want?"

He sighed dramatically. "It *wanted* you to forget about your past. That's what all this is about. Getting swallowed by the past. Human beings have a heck of a time living in the present."

"I know that," I said, relishing the renewed access to my storehouse of occult knowledge, so recently returned to me.

"Right now you're stuck in the 'you' of fifteen or sixteen years ago," he said. "The way you were during your marriage to Jenny. You haven't moved on. Neither have I. I'm stuck in my relationship with Celeste. I haven't moved on, even after all I've been through—even now, lying within an inch of my life.

"After we drew the attention of the thing behind reality, it tried to wipe clean the memory of our experience. In a way, it drove us both into marriages that, well, maybe we *thought* we wanted at the time, but only because it triggered our panic, our mental flight buttons."

"Forced us into fight or flight," I added.

"Exactly. Now that I'm dying, it's returned to finish the job, to swallow up the past and wipe our memories clean."

"Why does it want to do that?"

He shrugged. "That's what it does. The strangest thing is that it doesn't even realize it's doing it. It doesn't work that way. The thing just *is*; it doesn't think about stuff. It's like space, or time, or gravity: phenomena that exists and nobody knows why, or why they work the way they do. You wanna know something—" he leaned forward, giving me an intense gaze "—that, my friend, is the scariest part."

Just then the door opened. Annabelle stood at the threshold framed in wood and sunlight. "Good to see you catching up," she said.

"We decided to cruise down memory lane," James said.

She looked at me with a certain intimacy, a certain expectancy. No woman had looked at me that way in a long time.

"What time did you get up, Roger?" she asked. "It must've been early."

"Very," I said. "In fact I couldn't sleep, and when I came out here I saw James's light on."

She hummed disinterestedly. "Well it's about time for breakfast, eh boys? Would you like to give me a hand in the kitchen, Roger?"

"Sure thing." I stood for the first time in what seemed like hours. I glanced at James as I headed for the door, and he gave me a sinister, all-knowing smile. I realized it wasn't James who was looking at me. The thing behind reality was using him like a telescope, peering into the room from its great abyss through James's eyes. It made me shiver.

"I'll bring you up breakfast when it's done—" Annabelle said.

"When's Norma coming," he interrupted harshly. "I've got pain."

"Ten o'clock."

Silently he nodded, then curled up on the bed. The rustling of his sheets sounded like a rodent nuzzling in trash. He faced the wall, his back to us. Darkness settled over him.

Chapter Seven

As we made our way downstairs, Annabelle said, "Tell me honestly, how does he seem?"

I spoke without thinking. "Morbidly ill, insane. I think he's addicted to morphine."

I feared I'd spoken too bluntly, but her posture suddenly relaxed and she breathed a sigh of relief. "Thank God you see it too. I can't tell you how much better that makes me feel."

She cornered me at the bottom of the steps, pressing against me and leaning her head on my chest. It seemed she couldn't get enough of this cuddling and affection business—not that I minded. "Last night was… nice," she said, hugging me. I put my arms around her and stroked her long black hair.

"Is something going on between us?" I asked.

She laughed. "What's that supposed to mean? We'll let whatever happens happen and enjoy it. Why ruin everything by analyzing? Do you think you can do that—enjoy this? It's asking a lot from a bitter man."

She jabbed me playfully in the ribs. She'd said it as a joke, but it was one of those jokes that hit so close to home it came with a smack. Was I noticeably so bitter? Christ, I never wanted to be like that.

I softened my expression. "Yes, I can do that."

She smiled and craned her neck to kiss my nose. A quick, bird-like peck. I quivered at the sensation of her lips.

"What do you say we make breakfast together?" she asked.

"I'd love to."

"Great."

I followed her into the kitchen.

* * *

We spent most of the day together. It was strange, but for so long I had avoided women, and here I was clinging to one like a newborn. The way she spoke and the way she responded to me felt new and different. She never yelled or told me what to do. Of course, it was impossible for me to ignore some of the similarities she shared with Jenny… but even those were few, and forgivable.

James refused his breakfast on account of being exhausted, so Annabelle and I sat down at the kitchen table and we ate the meals we'd prepared for ourselves. We were becoming pros at this eating together game; it provided the best opportunities for intimacy. Later, when Norma showed up, I received a proper introduction.

"This is Roger Borough," Annabelle said, handing the woman a cup of coffee. "He and James were friends in college. Now he's come back to… spend some time with James."

Norma gave one quick nod. "Awfully kind of you to do that. Lord knows he needs it."

She wore blue scrubs and had a face mask and stethoscope dangling around her neck. Though middle-aged, her skin was smooth and unwrinkled, her hair thick and straight, tied back in a ponytail. She seemed soft, her full figure lending her a maternal quality.

"Pleased to meet you," I said, shaking her small hand.

"You guys old drinking buddies?" she asked.

I grinned. "Something like that. We lived the bachelor's life together for a while, until we both graduated and got married."

Norma glanced at Annabelle. "Would that be the, uh… Celeste woman?"

Annabelle nodded.

Norma shook her head and made a sound in her throat.

"Did I tell you she's missing?" Annabelle said.

"Missing? Nah. Do you mean *missing,* as in missing person—*CSI: New York, Law and Order*—that kind of missing?"

"Yes, that kind. That's where I was when you came over yesterday. The police called, asked to talk to James, but I told them he wasn't able to speak to anyone. They agreed to talk to me instead."

"And?"

She threw up her hands. "I went down to the police station and answered their questions, but I had no idea what to say. Celeste is missing, what do I care? Who knows the kind of trouble that bitch gets into."

"You're obviously sympathetic," Norma said with a smirk. "Was it enough for them? Or do they still want to speak to James?"

Annabelle sighed. "I don't know. I think my visit to the police station satisfied them for a while. But… if she doesn't turn up soon, I have the feeling they'll be poking their noses around."

Again, Norma shook her head. "A real shame what you people get up to out here in Brooklyn. Me, I prefer my safety—down near Jersey!"

I laughed out loud, but Annabelle sat there with that worried expression on her face.

"Good to see one of you has a sense of humor," she said, smiling at me. I went mushy all over. Her eyes were a brilliant reddish-brown and seemed to sparkle the harder I stared at them. For a moment I felt I could see into her, and I realized she was a woman of strange intelligence.

"I think I'll go check on the patient," she said, hurrying upstairs.

"She's nice," I said after she had gone.

Annabelle smiled. "I'm glad you like her." Then she took my hand. "But I'm even more glad you decided to stay for a while. I feel so much brighter just having you around. I had heard stories about people losing their marbles over caring for a sick relative, how much strain it puts on you, but I guess I didn't believe it. Still, I *know* I'm doing the right thing."

I squeezed her hand. "Whatever I can do to help, let me know."

She lowered her eyes. "That's very sweet. And I hate to do this—especially after the nice time we had last night—but all this has really put me behind. If you could just… I dunno, entertain yourself for a while so I can get some work done—"

"Say no more. I have an errand I need to run in the city. I was wondering if I could borrow your car again?"

"Yes, of course. But is it possible you could be back by six to give James his dinner? I'll make it, if you'll bring it to him. I'll take care of his lunch after Norma leaves around noon."

"Sure, no problem."

I sensed the layers of stress falling off her. She lifted her head, smiling now. "Wonderful, Roger. I get so nervous about my work, about getting buried. Even though I've been doing this a while, it's still a challenge. I'm totally independent and it's up to me to handle everything. When I was a nurse, there was a doctor to defer to and... these days it's just me. I have to take care of myself. This fucking golf project is a pain. I keep collecting emails from prospective clients, but I haven't had a chance to respond to them. If I don't soon, they'll find someone else—"

I stopped her by leaning forward and kissing the side of her mouth. It was spontaneous. I kept hearing the anxiety in her voice, how she kept feeding into it. My immediate impulse was to soothe her.

Worriment vacated her face and she gave me doe eyes. "Roger Borough, aren't you fresh," she said, imitating an English accent.

"A gentleman at your mercy," I replied.

The exchange pleased her; or perhaps the kiss itself had pleased her. She stood from the chair and very brazenly got in my lap. The warmth of our bodies mixed, driving up my heart rate. I put my arms around her waist, the ends of her long black hair tickling my skin. Then she bent and kissed me. Nothing modest, nothing timid; a full-on, mouth-to-mouth, sappy-as-hell smoocher.

It felt so foreign. How long had it been? Not really since Jenny. A few stolen bar-kisses here and there while I was drunk, but nothing like this. I thought I had forgotten how to do it, but I soon realized it was like riding a bicycle.

We sat kissing passionately for several minutes, the quiet house surrounding us, morning sun streaming through the kitchen window above the sink. Her tongue quested through my mouth, and I put my fingers in her luxurious hair.

A loud noise upstairs ended the moment. James, yelling, words garbled with anger.

"What's that?" I said.

Annabelle appeared unfazed. Smiling, she got out of my lap and straightened her clothes. "He always yells when Norma puts him in the bath. It's a game he plays. He claims it's such an outrage to be treated like a baby, but on the other hand he likes it when Norma pays attention to him."

"Oh."

There was a pause. I could still hear James's shouting. I listened, thinking about the thing behind reality, whether it occupied James's body during moments like this.

"I liked kissing," Annabelle said.

I smiled at her. "Me too. Very much. Best kiss of my whole life."

She laughed. "Don't get carried away. I'm off to get a jump on work." She started for the stairs.

"Okay. Oh—I meant to ask you. Is there a computer with internet?"

"In the living room. Be sure to turn it off when you're done. What's the errand you have to run?"

I thought about lying, but realized it would probably be a bad move. Instead I decided to tell her without explaining. "I have to find a bookstore," I said. "One that specializes in the occult."

To my surprise, she merely nodded and continued upstairs.

Chapter Eight

According to Google, there were only two bookstores in New York dealing in rare manuscripts and specialty occult texts. One was in Albany. The other, fortunately, was in Manhattan, Hell's Kitchen area. I pulled up the directions on my smartphone, got in Annabelle's car, and headed for the city.

I tried to remember the title of the book we had used to summon the thing behind reality. My memory was blurry, though bits and pieces had begun to return. Apart from the Ohio State library, I recalled the little used bookstore on the eastside of Columbus I liked to frequent. It was strange how deeply this memory had submerged in my unconscious, surfacing only now after my conversation with James.

Randolf's Rare Books, I reflected, *owned by that buzzardly old lunatic Randolf. He was the one to help me understand the more complex aspects of occultism.*

The two of us spent hours talking, discussing the various spells I was casting around campus. Randolf was a good listener, and he knew more about the occult than anyone. For a while, he was like a second father figure to me. He didn't practice any of the occult arts himself, yet he was never surprised when I recounted my successes to him. He regarded matters of the supernatural with a kind of banal acceptance, which I had found both confusing and impressive.

Randolf would've died long ago, and so there was no hope of ever contacting him. I'd run a Google search on his bookstore, and the listing came back closed. There was a phone number, but it led to a *We're sorry, the number you have dialed is no longer in service* message. It seemed the days of *Randolf's Rare Books* had come to an end.

But I remained hopeful that seeing the book again might jog my memory about the ritual we performed. Still, there was no guarantee. The bookstore near Hell's Kitchen most likely wouldn't carry what I was looking for, even if I could remember the book's name. At the very least, however, I could pick up *some* kind of occult book to help me fill in the gaps.

As the stream of traffic entered the tunnel leading to Manhattan, the light became halved. I switched on the headlights. Still dazed, I coasted through the concrete corridor on autopilot, letting my hands do the driving. Dimly glowing artificial lights passed overhead, blurring together in a continuous glare.

I probed the inner regions of my mind, interrogating memories, analyzing images, and examining thoughts. I attempted to uncover whatever events my unconscious had repressed from the period surrounding my college years. The deeper I dug, the more I seemed to uncover.

Jesus. It feels like I've forgotten half my life.

I emerged from the tunnel and the sunlight struck me so brightly I was momentarily blind. Mechanically, I switched off the headlights, reducing my speed. The buildings and structures of Manhattan distinguished themselves from the glare, and I happened to glance in the rearview mirror—to find Jenny sitting in the backseat.

"Hello, Roger," she said.

My heart stopped, panic flooding me. I nearly lost control of the wheel. I had to slam on the brakes, almost rear-ending the car up ahead, and then the car behind me began honking. In true New York fashion the driver stuck his head out the window as he roared past, yelling, "What's yah problem, asshole?"

I closed my eyes, reminding myself to breathe. *Relax, take deep breaths, visualize calm. There's no one in the backseat.*

That worked until I opened my eyes again and saw Jenny sitting, not in the backseat now, but right next to me up front, so close I could reach out and touch her.

"Jesus!"

She grinned. "No. But you're close."

She wasn't the young Jenny anymore. She was older, closer to my age. Her skin had grooves and the hint of wrinkles, and there was a slight yellow to her complexion.

"Good thing you're not really there," I said. "Because you're finally starting to look your age."

She chuckled. "Thanks, same to you. I felt you were ready to see me as I truly am instead of that glamorized image you've kept locked inside your head for however-many years. I've aged, Roger, same as you. That's what time does to people."

"Don't lecture me about time." I felt the anger rising in my throat, and I marveled at how quickly it could sneak up on me again. "I don't think time has been as cruel to you as it has me. Fourteen years since you left, Jenny. I've spent all of them alone. Do you know how lonely it is just to even say that? I don't imagine you experienced it the same way."

"Oh, Roger. Still as bitter as always. I think you'll be surprised to learn I too was lonely." She performed the familiar mannerism of whipping her blonde hair out of her eyes. Seeing her do this sent shivers down my spine. It'd been a long time, yet I remembered it vividly.

She still looks beautiful, too.

"Sure, I had a string of lovers," she continued. "Being a therapist is great for that. You meet a bunch of screwed up people who know nothing about love and only how to fuck."

"You slept with your patients?" I was appalled, but not totally surprised.

"Damn straight. Dozens. But I never remarried." She seemed to become sad after saying this. "Don't let anyone fool you, therapists are as screwed up as the patients coming in through the doors."

"I'll remember that," I said.

The traffic started flowing and I accelerated to keep up.

"What the hell do you want?"

"It isn't just what *I* want." She glared at me until I assented to look over and then proceeded to stare me down with her pretty blue eyes. I didn't see Jenny in those eyes anymore. Whatever looked out was dead and lifeless, nonexistent, empty, and went on forever.

And when she spoke, she no longer sounded human but like a machine, a frequency, a TV screen gone fuzzy. "It's what *we* want." She gave me a sinister wink, opening her mouth fathoms too wide, resembling some kind of demon or flesh-eating zombie. She began climbing onto the seat.

"*We* want to devour every piece of your existence," she said. "Your body, your soul, and your mind. The space you occupy in the universe, the accumulation of time you experienced, the memories you collected, the thoughts you had—all of it must be consigned to the abyss, the void of creation, where you'll be ground up, diffused, and spit back as a bug, a rock, a mote of space dust in the middle of nowhere. This marks the end of you, Roger Borough. It's time you move to the next stage of your existence..."

The cab of the vehicle filled with a deafening, rushing wind, a *whoosh* like the inside of a tornado. Although I didn't actually *feel* this wind, I heard it in my ears, moving up the pipeline to my brain, like an insect boring into my skull. I tried to scream but nothing came out. All I heard was *whooshing*. I had enough sense to pull over, but even this was dangerous, as I wound up cutting across two lanes, yielding honks and shouts from other drivers.

Jenny was on her hands and knees, inching toward me at an excruciating pace, her mouth hanging almost to the seat. For a moment, I imagined she was an oversized cat, hissing, getting ready to pounce.

When I looked, my heart turned to ice. I could see the horrible darkness spewing from her mouth like fog or mist, blotting out everything it touched. Miniature stars and planets twinkled in the depths, growing larger and brighter by the second.

I unlatched my seatbelt, opening the driver side door ready to flee into the traffic. But the moment I allowed exterior reality to enter the cab, that horrendous *whooshing* dissipated and the image of Jenny flickered out, taking the encroaching blackness with it.

I sat shaking, adjusting to the sound of cars. I felt queasy, and so I leaned out the door to vomit. I had been roused from a fever dream. My skin felt cold. My head throbbed.

Get a grip, I told myself. *Come on, man, you're losing it and this thing's only just begun.*

I closed the door, wiping my face with my hands. In a little while I felt relaxed, and so I pulled the car onto the road and merged with the traffic. But every so often I checked the backseat to make sure no one was there.

Chapter Nine

The occult bookstore was called *Cosmos, Psyche, and Higher Worlds.* After scoring a parking spot, I searched around for the entrance. The door was secreted behind the back of a larger building, partially visible from the street.

To keep things hidden, I thought, as I opened the door and stepped inside. I was met by a long room lined with bookshelves. Overhanging chandeliers, the old iron type from around the Victorian era, illuminated many leather volumes. The floor was covered with paperbacks and sprawling disordered piles containing history's long line of bestsellers.

The shop appeared empty, but as I approached the counter I noticed a metal call bell. I struck it, sending a shrilly *ding* through the aisles. Behind the counter was a collection of labeled jars containing herbs. The names sounded foreign; however, I seemed to remember that I knew them once, back in college.

In addition to the jars, a row of wood filing cabinets sat against the wall. Atop these were card catalog cabinets, the kind once used by libraries. From behind a red curtain between the filing cabinets and jars, a teenage boy emerged wearing black. His face was sallow, pockmarked with acne, dominated in the center by a thinly growing premature mustache. His hair was wild, unkempt, and brown as a forest tree.

"Yes?" he said. "Can I help you?"

He sounded American, but with an underlying Eastern European accent.

"I'm looking for something in particular," I said. "A book. An old book. But I can't recall the name. Is there someone here I could talk to?"

He nodded, then over his shoulder: "Papa! Come!" Looking at me, he added, "My Father is the owner. He will assist." The boy moved from behind the counter out into the labyrinth of books and began organizing some paperbacks on the floor.

A moment later an enormous man stepped through the curtain, so big he seemed to dwarf the entire shop. He resembled his son in that he had wild brown hair and a thin mustache. When he looked at me, I was struck by the intense blueness of his eyes, like peering into a cloudless sky.

"Yes?" he said, his accent thick and strong. "Is there something specific you need that my son Sergei could not help you find?"

"There is actually." I realized I didn't know how or where to begin. If I told this man about my past, would he think I was crazy?

This is an occult bookstore, after all, I told myself. *The guy probably hears stories like yours all the time.*

True, but I was already clamming up, sweating, my heart pounding in my chest. The longer I stared into the man's alien eyes, the more I felt transfixed.

He regarded me queerly, cocking his head somewhat to the right, his pupils gazing at me like spotlights. *Holy shit,* I thought, *is he reading my mind?*

Then he broke into a grin, laughing, belly heaving as he wagged his finger at me. "You want to tell me something, don't you? You're afraid. I can see just by looking at you." He called over to his son. "Sergei. Do you see how afraid?"

"Yes, Papa."

"Even my son sees!" He stuck out his hand. "There is nothing to be afraid of, sir."

His sudden gregariousness put me at ease. I laughed and shook his hand. His grip was big and strong, and he used it to pump my hand enthusiastically.

He moved around the counter to join me. "My name is Alexander Maninov," he said. "This is my son, Sergei."

"I'm Roger," I replied.

"Glad to meet you, Roger," Alexander said. "What can I assist you with?"

I gathered up my resolve. "Well, I have a very strange story I would like to tell, something most people would find crazy. I'm worried you won't believe me."

He exploded into riotous laughter. "To think!" he said. "Afraid of being called crazy in a bookstore owned by a Russian warlock who is *most* arguably insane. Think about that—think about it *rationally*."

I thought about it; chuckled. "I see what you mean."

"'Course you do! Now, tell me everything. I'll do my best to assist finding whatever you need."

I didn't exactly tell him *everything*. Even his agreeable brand of gregariousness could not put me totally at ease. But I revealed much, including my experiences in college, what I recalled of the strange ritual James and I performed to summon the thing behind reality, and the book where I had discovered the ritual. I told him of James's brain tumor—how, following a seemingly normal life, he had suddenly consigned himself to terminal illness without so much as a raised finger. I reported that the *thing* had somehow entered James, was using him to gain access to our world.

Alexander listened with profound eagerness. When I finished, I was certain he would call me a loony toon and tell me to get lost. But instead he showed signs of genuine interest, placing his hand on my shoulder, saying, "You are in terrible danger, friend Roger." He made a *tick* sound in his throat. "Things of this nature are not to be toyed with, especially by a couple of college kids."

He gave me a disapproving but sympathetic glare, then bade me follow him into the rows of books. "Tell me what you remember," he said, scanning the bindings with his fingers.

"But that's just it, I remember very little. Most of my memories are resurfacing now in dreams."

"Perhaps you should hypnotize yourself, ever thought of that?"

"No." I explained to him how the more I got involved in this, the more memories became accessible, as if the experience was dredging them up. I attempted to recount in fullness that night on the Ohio State campus. Alexander nodded, drawing certain books from the shelves, but each time he showed me a title, I shook my head. None of the books sounded familiar.

We moved farther into the aisles. Every so often Alexander asked his son a question in Russian and they'd hunt down a book. But after an hour, we'd come up with nothing.

I sighed. "I knew this wouldn't be easy."

"Just don't lose hope," Alexander encouraged me. "I still have a few tricks up my sleeve."

He yelled for Sergei to keep watch on the store, then escorted me behind the counter, indicating something about his private collection. We passed through the red curtain and down a wooden staircase.

At the bottom was a single room, the size of a studio apartment. It was lit by an antique lamp that cast its glow across a desk scattered with papers, various books, and a glass display case housing peculiar items. Opposite the case, a double bed sat heaped with dirty linens.

"Sergei and I sleep down here," Alexander explained, almost self-consciously. "But we do have an apartment in the city, too."

I peered in the glass case, admiring the oddities within: a collection of gems, old crystals, fossilized flora and fauna, a dissected snake, even a shrunken head.

"Katya, my wife, died six years ago," Alexander said. "Sergei has been motherless since."

"I'm sorry to hear that."

"Yes, it's a wound that doesn't heal, no matter what I do about it. It has become, for me, my personal Chiron."

He approached the wall, scooting aside a wood cabinet to reveal a metal safe. "This is where I keep my treasured relics." He dialed in the combination and the hatch popped open. His hands disappeared into the wall, rummaging, and reappeared holding a slender glass bottle.

"Kubanskaya vodka," he said, unscrewing the top and taking a hearty swig. He passed it to me, then went back to digging in the safe.

The liquor had a cool, pleasant taste, with a mild hint of lemon. Immediately it put me in a sort of catatonic state. I was forced to lean against the wall for support. I capped the bottle and set it on the ground. Too much of that and I wouldn't be able to make it back to Brooklyn.

"Ah, here it is," Alexander said, producing a black leather book. He read off the title, which sounded like Latin. I shook my head. It wasn't the book I remembered. He repeated this process a number of times, the books becoming more sinister, eldritch, and rare, but nothing resembled the book from my past.

Alexander stood quietly, thinking. Then he said, "Did you know I never plan on remarrying?"

The question caught me off guard. "I didn't know that."

"'Tis true. After Katya, what's the use? No woman will be like her. She was an angel, a goddess from above. She was *Russian*. These New York girls, they are more like demons than women. They'd kill me with their love before nurturing me with it." He stopped, retrieved the vodka, and started drinking.

"I sometimes think like that," I said.

His brows rose. "Is your wife dead?"

"No. But she divorced me, so it was kind of like a death. I decided I didn't want to be with another woman, partly because no other woman would be Jenny, partly because I was so mad she left. I didn't want to risk getting hurt again."

He gave me a discerning eye, passing the vodka. I didn't refuse but I sipped it slowly. *He's reading my mind again,* I thought.

"Not *quite* the same," he remarked. "But yes, we're similar. Tell me, do you still feel this way?"

I started to answer when suddenly an image of Annabelle entered my mind. I recalled the night I spent in her bed. The slow dreamy wash of her black hair, the feeling of her skin, how she had gotten into my lap and kissed me. I smiled.

Alexander said, "What's this? Why do you smile?"

"I just realized something."

"What?"

"I realized I *don't* feel that way anymore. At least, not completely."

"No? What changed your mind?"

"A woman—Annabelle."

"The girl with whom your friend is staying?"

I nodded. "She and I have been getting… close. And it feels great. Those fourteen years of isolation and bitterness rinse away each time she touches me. She isn't like other women, those demons you mentioned. She's kind, honest, and sincere. I think she genuinely likes me."

"You sound in love."

This made me laugh. "Maybe. But whatever it is, it's… *changing* me. I can feel that, like I'm becoming… someone else."

"Interesting. I should be so lucky to meet such a woman."

"She's something, all right."

"And your friend?"

"Who, James? I don't think he minds. He's happy Annabelle and I have gotten together."

Alexander swigged from the bottle. "That isn't what I meant. I meant do you think he'll live?"

"Live?" It was a moment before I could register the concept. "No, I don't think he'll live."

"But don't you *want* him to live? Don't you care?"

"Of course I care. It's just… well, he himself said he was going to die." Then I had this sudden thought: What if James could be saved with occult magic? It hadn't occurred to me to consider that until now. Should my newfound joy come at the expense of my friend's death? There had to be another way.

"I want him to live," I said. Then, more heartfelt: "*I don't want him to die.*"

Alexander scratched his scruffy chin. His blue eyes burned into me. "That is good to hear. You know, it's possible you don't need the book. Words and symbols are of little importance in the realm of the occult. It's all a big trick. They are the representation of a thing, not the thing itself. They are not the substance."

"But it was the book that enabled James and I to do the summoning all those years ago," I said.

Alexander shook his head. "You only think it was the book. The words were just the external trigger. What if I told you the ritual—the actual summoning—you accomplished within yourself? What if I made the claimed that the book was as insignificant as a blade of grass?"

"I see where you're going, but then how did we—"

"All magic, all *otherness*, is generated by the self. By the infinite. No books, no spells, no esoteric doctrine—nothing but the self can manifest reality. You could have had a Webster's dictionary with you that night. You could achieve the same results."

"I'm not that powerful."

His gaze became piercing. I thought it might punch right through me. "Yes," he said, "you are."

There was a long pause. Alexander drank his vodka. I was thinking about words being symbols for things. It reminded me of what Randolf used to tell me, that images could be granted reality or divested of it, based upon the spirituality of the magician.

The word *God* began to revolve inside my head. What did a person mean when they said *God?* Did they mean an old bearded man looking down from heaven? Did they mean emptiness, a void from which all things could manifest? Did they mean a black hole, a star, a sun? My idea of God could never be the same as another's idea of God. And although they could listen to my idea, and perhaps understand it, they could never know what it was like *experiencing my own idea of God*. The more I thought about it, the more I understood how immaterial the book really was. I didn't need words, symbols someone else had arranged in order to convey their own experience. Everything I needed was inside of *me*.

"You're getting it," Alexander said, breaking my train of thought. "Now you see you don't need books or spells or fancy incantations. You only need your spirit, your soul, your self—your personal experience. No amount of magic can replace that."

I looked at him, thunderstruck. "You *are* reading my mind."

He shrugged. "Told you I was a warlock. But now, what about your friend? You say you want him to live. How will you accomplish that? He is the key. He is the one close to death. That *other* is using him to access our world."

"I do want James to live, but he seems resigned to die. I feel like he wants it to swallow him up so that it can eradicate him, like he gets some morbid satisfaction out of it."

"That's because he does. For whatever reason, your friend has gone over to the dark side, and the only way he can be brought back is if he *chooses* to be brought back. In other words, he must decide he wants to live."

His words hung in the room. I listened to the hollow *plink-plunk* of Alexander working down the dregs of his vodka. Finally he said, "In order for you to have any success with your friend, you must help him find the will to live. Can you do that?"

I struggled with my answer. "It's hard to say. He's always had a better life than me, the life I thought I wanted. He got the girls. He had the happy marriage—at least for a while. He got the successful career. Then—out of nowhere—illness, impending death. Doesn't make sense."

"But there's something there." Alexander eyed me keenly, betraying the influence of the alcohol. "Something he's not telling you, some reason he wishes to die. Get him to tell you that, then you're on your way to inspiring him to live. Once you get that far…" He rummaged through the contents of the safe, handing me a business card—"You call Li Xi."

I looked at the card—bone-white with black calligraphic script—and three black Chinese characters across the top. Below were the words *Li Xi*. Below that *Esoteric Acupuncturist, Master of Oriental Medicine, Spiritual Healer*. There was a number, but no address.

"What's this?"

"That's who's going to help save your friend's life, once you get him to open his mind a little. Trust me, Li Xi is a wizard of the soul. He can accomplish things that you'd label miracles, simply because there are no words for it."

"You make him sound like Jesus."

"I've seen it with my own eyes. You call him when you're ready, tell him Alexander Maninov referred you. But only once you've gotten to the bottom of your friend's disposition, once you've gotten him to *change* the way he's thinking. Then call Li Xi."

I stared at the card, entranced by it. It could have been a jewel from a distant alien planet, a fossil from the bottom of the ocean, that's how fantastic it seemed. *Esoteric Acupuncture?* Who'd ever heard of such a thing? Not me, not even with my newly remembered catalogue of occult information.

Calmly, I thanked Alexander and slid the card into my wallet. We headed upstairs.

We said goodbye warmly as I made my departure, agreeing to keep in touch. I bought a book on esoteric acupuncture almost as a show of faith, using some of my dwindling pocket money from my teaching job. Then I left the store, got into the car, and headed for Brooklyn.

It was going on five o'clock.

* * *

On the drive back, I decided I would get to the bottom of James's illness—whether he liked it or not. And I'd start with his separation from Celeste.

Chapter Ten

The house seemed empty and dark when I returned. The sun was sinking behind the buildings, throwing a purple sheet of twilight over the neighborhood. The cars on the street had their headlights on, a zigzag of gold beams.

I stepped inside and called hello, but nobody answered. The house was pitch-dark. When I flipped the switch in the hall, the luminescence felt like an intrusion.

I walked into the kitchen, flipping on more lights, and poured a glass of orange juice after setting my acupuncture book on the counter. Somebody had clearly eaten something since a pile of dirty dishes lay in the sink. I checked my watch: quarter past six.

Annabelle had asked that I return by six to serve James his dinner, which she was going to prepare. I was running a little late, but I assumed she had gotten wrapped up in her work and was running late too; that would explain the deserted house. I saw no sign of James's dinner set out. Perhaps I'd have to make one for him.

I sat down at the table, drinking my juice, trying to decide a course of action to take. The vodka I'd sampled had left me tired and listless, and I suddenly wanted nothing more than to curl up in Annabelle's bed and go to sleep.

Then I heard a sound that at first I thought was coming from the window above the sink. It was a barely audible hiss. I tried to ignore it, thinking the sound just some natural noise of nature, odd only because it was isolated in the kitchen. Perhaps it was a car getting a flat tire out on the street or an airplane cruising overhead on its way to LaGuardia.

When it persisted—and more, when it began to amplify—I took an active interest. The hiss filled the room, coming from everywhere and nowhere: from the walls, the window, the ceiling. It grew louder, seeming to funnel inward on itself, becoming more of a word than a sound—

—"ssss… Roger… sss," the hiss said. "Ssss… *hey Roger, sss, look up here,* sss..."

I was stunned. I'd gotten used to some strange shit—dead ex-wives, lucid dreams, mind-reading, cosmic demons—but for some reason, hearing this alien sound utter my name sent me over the edge.

I shut my eyes, flooded with an infantile rage, and threw my head back. "No, I won't hear it! I can't take it anymore. Leave me alone!"

But the hissing chuckled, the sound of a machine imitating laughter. *"Ssss... Aw, come on Roger, sss, don't you want to play?"*

"No!" I shouted back instantly. However, I found my eyes opening. No matter how much I wanted to refuse, the reality of the situation wouldn't go away, not until I dealt with it.

James was up on the ceiling. Well, his face was on the ceiling, a distorted version of it anyway, eyes full of mischief and rage, hair the color of iron. A face moving in liquid animation, drifting back and forth like the disembodied Cheshire cat, teeth all a-grin.

Through the racket of electro-interference, he said, *"Ssss... I think you'll want to come up here, Roger, sss... I've got your lovey-dovey here, she's all tied up, sss..."* It was James's voice undoubtedly, but alien, inhuman.

A quick image flashed across the ceiling, projected onto it like the screen of an old drive-in movie. Annabelle lassoed to a chair, gagged, two dark shapes looming around her—*Jenny and Celeste*—followed by James's hooded eyes and widening smile. My heart froze.

"Annabelle!" I cried, shooting up from the chair. James's wicked laughter pursued me out of the kitchen, down the hall, up the stairs. It was like he had possessed the very house itself, all the boards, nails, and drywall. I flipped the hall light and it snapped on with a *pop*, showering sparks everywhere. I rushed to James's bedroom and threw open the door.

Inside, it was so dark that at first I imagined I had opened a portal to outer space. Tiny gold flecks hung in the air, revolving in place, glittering like dust motes caught in afternoon sun. I felt a distinctly real presence. The air seemed to breathe, to swell with energy, producing the electricity I'd heard in the kitchen.

"Ssss... come on in, Roger, sss... Don't be afraid. And please, sss... shut the door."

I did as he said, and immediately the glittering motes of light sucked together, condensing until they formed a neat, tight orb. This orb, burning yellow and gold, became the main source of illumination in the room.

From my island of blackness I could see James's bed in the corner. He was there, sitting up with a sheet pulled to his waist. The sight of him shocked me. He looked like a demon, some ghoul of the graves, his skin sunken and haggard, smudged with large blemishes. His eyes shone out of his head, like two oncoming headlights, set in his cadaverous face, which now displayed a wide accordion of yellow-bone teeth.

"My God," I said. "What happened to you?"

He tipped forward, leaning into a bow, as if to show off the massive hole in the top of his skull. A jagged section of his scalp had been removed, making his head look like a jack-o-lantern with the crown cut out.

From this hole sprung the geyser of liquid blackness that had pooled around the room. I had to look closely, and when I did I saw the blackness *streaming*, like a forest creek, a blackness indeed organic, a living presence in the room. It took only a second to understand who that being was.

"It's here," I said. "Isn't it?"

He leaned back, taking that wretched chasm from my sight. I didn't need him to answer. I knew this wasn't James I was addressing. James was as good as dead.

What I looked upon was the thing behind reality. The Time Eater. The cosmic entity James and I summoned on the Ohio State campus twenty years ago.

And it was staring at me.

"Ssss... I feel great," he said. "Who knew dying could be this much fun, sss...?"

"You're not James," I said. "You're that thing, that blind spot. You're nothing. You can't feel great. You don't feel anything."

"I feel the *deepest*," he said. "I feel the worst of the worst... sss... and I feel the best of the best. Right now I feel euphoric, do you wanna know why—sss..."

His voice oscillated between James's and the alien's, creating a kind of schizophrenic hybrid. Before I had a chance to answer, he thrust his arms out in mock crucifixion, a pose humorously self-conscious in its sincerity. Up and down his forearms were dozens of syringes, needles jabbed in his flesh, stubby rubber ends sticking out firmly with trickles of blood flowing from the veins.

"*Morphine, sss...!*" he exclaimed, rattling his body and shaking the quill of hypodermic needles.

I realized my mouth was hanging open. Closing it, I said, "Where did you get all those?"

He shrugged. "Norma, the nurse lady. Who else? I like her best. She's so soft, gentle, and kind. She takes care of me because no one else will. Sometimes... sss... I think she has a crush on me, sss..."

That sounds just like the old James. James and his stupid magic mommy fantasies about finding the perfect woman, all those girls he had in college, which culminated in Celeste, and yet none had ever satisfied him.

I wanted to interview James about his childhood, specifically about his mother, to find out anything related to his willful desire to die. But first, I had to make sure Annabelle was safe.

"She's over there," he said, reading my thoughts. The glowing orb that had settled in the middle of the room glided a few feet to the left, illuminating the area by the closet. The door was open, a menacing crack of darkness revealing two pairs of watchful red eyes.

Celeste and Jenny, crouching in there like a pair of voyeurs at a sex show.

My attention didn't linger because directly in front of the door was a chair occupied by a frightened, trembling form, her soft pale skin gleaming, her black hair hanging over the back.

"Annabelle!" I rushed to untie her. She'd been gagged. The knots binding her to the chair were messy, childlike in their clumsiness. As I worked to free her, I heard soft chitters and snickers from the women in the closet, and, reaching over with my leg, I kicked the door closed.

Annabelle stared at me with wide, beseeching eyes. When I finally got the gag out of her mouth, she screamed—a sound that rocketed through the house. James began laughing his sick, psychotic laugh, and the sounds merged together until both became one. I thought my ears would explode from the chaos.

I scooped Annabelle into my arms, crossing the room in less than five strides, opening the door to the hall, escaping through it, slamming it, still hearing James's haunting laughter fading on the opposite end.

We made it to her bedroom and I placed her gently on the bed, making sure her door was shut and locked. She was breathing rapidly, her chest undulating in exasperated movements. Her eyes gazed toward the ceiling as I grabbed a half-full water bottle from the nightstand and handed it to her.

She muttered a halfhearted protest, so I unscrewed the top and held it to her lips. She drank timidly, but gradually the composure returned to her face. I positioned a pillow behind her head, stroking her stomach.

"Tell me everything," I said.

She paused as a tiny flicker of rebellion passed through her eyes.

She's so scared, I thought. *She doesn't understand what's happening. Probably thinks I have something do with it.*

She's right.

"Everything's okay," I assured her. "You can trust me."

She proceeded to have a pure, unadulterated, emotional release, her mouth twisting in a hoop of terror as she seized the water bottle from my hands, crunching it in her frantic grip, then hurling it against the wall.

"Oh... *God...*" she wailed.

She broke into tears and a frenzied account of how she'd come to be tied up in the chair. Every so often, whatever she was describing became too much, and then she'd sob until she could continue. In order to get the whole story, I had to pay close attention.

She had been lured away from her computer earlier that afternoon, in a situation not unlike my experience in the kitchen. She'd heard James's voice calling to her. When she'd gotten up to investigate, she found James out of bed, standing by the closet with the door ajar, peering inside. She could only see his back, and yet she understood immediately that something was wrong; most likely, he was high on morphine again and spacing out. Norma was there that morning, so he was probably experiencing the side effects.

She approached with the intent of helping him back into bed, when all at once a giant shadow passed over the room. That was how she described it, as a shadow.

She glanced at the window, thinking a cloud had gotten in front of the sun, but she was shocked to see total darkness outside, and this at four-thirty in the afternoon. Suddenly, all light drained from the room, and she even thought—as crazy as it sounded—that stars and planets were twinkling all about her, like she had stepped into outer space.

Hands came out of the black to seize her. She was so out of her wits that they managed to force her into the chair, gag, and bind her. The fear had rendered her docile, a scared and confused child who would be led anywhere.

But when she realized she was being restrained, she started to struggle. She tried to scream, but no sound came out. She looked up and standing over her in the dark was James's ex-wife, Celeste, and some other woman, a blonde.

Jenny.

Annabelle became hysterical as she recounted this part of the story, claiming the women didn't look real, that they were "distorted," she said, and sickly pale. Like corpses. They grinned at her, pawing her shoulders and breasts with curled bony fingers.

She was so overwhelmed with what she was seeing that she passed out and didn't regain consciousness until I burst into the room.

Once she had finished, I helped her take in long deep breaths and stroked the side of her head. Eventually she relaxed. She looked up at me with silent appreciation, her eyes conveying the *thank you* her lips could not emit. I nodded, letting her know she didn't need to say anything.

Later, we went downstairs to have a drink and something to eat. As we passed the closed door of James's bedroom, Annabelle's hand went ice-cold in my grip.

I got her seated at the table and poured us both a glass of brandy I'd selected from the liquor cabinet. We took a moment to sip it down as the house thrummed with eerie silence.

"Feels like a dream," she said. "Was Celeste really there? Did it really happen?"

"It happened. It's been happening since I arrived."

She lifted her eyebrows. "It has?"

"Uh-huh."

"Tell me. I want the whole story, Roger Borough, so don't spare me because you think I'm delicate or some nonsense. I want to know everything or I'll toss you out on your ass."

I laughed. She made it sound like we were a real couple, like we had lived together for years. "All right," I said, taking a sip of brandy. "I'll tell."

We passed three hours at that table, finishing the liquor bottle, and by the end we were both tipsy. The night grew darker in the window and every so often we'd hear a thump coming from James's bedroom.

He's listening to us, I thought, seeing the image of his sick, twisted form pressed against the floor, ear buried in the carpet.

I told Annabelle everything, starting with my experiences at Ohio State. I went through the ritual, Jenny, my marriage, the Time Eater, my experiences since I had arrived there—all the way up to Li Xi's business card, which Alexander had given me earlier that day. When I finished, Annabelle's face was pale, like she was feeling nauseous.

"What do you think?" I said.

She shook her head. "I don't know what to think."

"But you believe me?"

She paused. I thought she would say no. But instead she nodded, weakly. "I believe you. I must. At least you gave me some explanation. Without that, I think I would go completely insane."

"And don't forget, you experienced it firsthand tonight."

She nodded. "I did. I've been trying to forget it."

"Don't, you've gotten this far! You can anchor me. Or else I'll be the one going insane."

She closed her eyes, reached her arms above her head, and yawned. "I'm exhausted. I could sleep for weeks."

"Must be the brandy."

She gave a dopey smile, then sort of batted her eyelashes at me, Betty Boop style. "Care to join me for a thousand year nap?"

I had become entranced by her hair, marveling at how it slithered snakelike off her shoulders, pooling at the small of her back. It was magnificent. I stood, fumbling with the chair (brandy), and stuck out my hand. "Let's get you upstairs."

She grinned, her face imbued with a coquettish luster. "What about you?"

"I'll be taking a rain check, I'm afraid. I have a long night ahead of me. James and I have some talking to do."

Her lips curled into a pout and she emitted a single word *"Boo"* like an indignant child. I found the action to be so irresistibly cute that I looped my arms around her and kissed the side of her cheek.

"You can kiss me somewhere else, if you like," she said.

Her words produced a throbbing in my groin. My heart accelerated. Whenever we were affectionate it felt like a dream. I still couldn't believe this was happening.

But then I caught a whiff of the brandy on her breath, and with it came a sober dose of conscience. So much had happened—it was taking a toll on her. On top of that, she was drunk. It didn't seem right. I'd be taking advantage of her.

I backed off.

She recognized my change in attitude instantly and made another of those infantile pouty noises. "Okay," she said, "fine, a rain check. I'm super tired anyway."

"Up we go, then—" I leaned down and hoisted her out of the chair. I felt a small pain in my lower back but was able to ignore it with the aid of the alcohol. She laughed, casting her arms around my neck, letting me carry her like a bride.

"Am I too heavy?" she said, kissing my neck.

"No, I've got you."

We reached the landing and passed down the hall. As we did there was a loud thump on the other side of James's door. Annabelle jumped and nearly screamed, clinging to me like a scared child, her face pressed against my chest.

We entered her room and I laid her on the bed. All coquetry had vanished and she'd gone pale once more. I helped her out of her clothes, averting my eyes in a gentlemanly fashion. She got herself snugly under the covers and looked up at me with hooded eyes, drifting in and out of sleep.

"Get some rest," I said.

"But..." She pointed to James's bedroom.

"Don't worry. I'll keep him busy. If you need anything, holler."

"Thanks, Roger." She shifted onto her side, showing me her shoulder, and fell asleep.

On my way out I hit the lights, consigning the room to darkness. Annabelle called out in a small, terrified voice, "No! Leave it on!"

I flipped the switch back on, closing the door behind me.

Chapter Eleven

What the hell is he doing in there?

The low succession of thuds vibrated the carpet beneath my feet. The door rattled gently. Every so often the handle turned left-right, left-right.

I imagined James, or perhaps one of his female sidekicks, raving in the room and running aimlessly from one end to the other, like a mental patient in a padded cell.

He's like a rat in a cage. Anytime now he'll start gnawing off his own feet. Maybe he already has.

I waited for the noises to stop, standing nervously in the dark hall. When it was quiet, I entered the bedroom.

Blackness, a vast bottomless ocean, greeted me at the threshold. I couldn't see a thing. I groped for the light switch, tried it, *nothing*.

"Jesus fucking Christ," I muttered.

A blinding flash of illumination and there was James, nestled in bed, the sheet up to his waist, in his horribly stained t-shirt. The glow reminded me of one of those Chinese globe lamps as it hovered above his head.

"*Who*?" he said. The word emerged from his throat like a wheeze. His face had become unrecognizable. The skin was pale and leathery beneath his haggard five o'clock shadow. Eyes, droopy as an old mutt's, yet startlingly intense, peered through the dark.

The chair beside the closet slid across the floor of its own accord, coming to a rest before the bed. "Sit," he said. "I can see you have a lot on your mind."

I crossed the room, scanning the darkness for any sign of Celeste and Jenny. I saw only distant shimmering stars and glowing planets. The closet, too, seemed lost, absorbed in the impenetrable dark. I had the feeling both girls were in there, though, locked away like beasts.

I sat in the chair and James did a very strange thing: he turned his nose up, sniffing, then said, "Been drinking? Just like old times." He hooked a finger toward Annabelle's room. "Did it do the trick? Did you get yourself a piece of that? Tell me *all* about it. Tell me how you fucked her and yanked that long ebony hair."

My anger erupted, but I swallowed it down. I knew that was just what he wanted—to get a rise out of me. I'd have to cool my jets if I hoped to be successful at this.

"Sounds like you're jealous," I said.

He scoffed, and I swore I saw a blast of brown miasma vacate his mouth. "You've got to be kidding. I could have had her years ago. She's always had a thing for me, since we were kids. I could've fucked her anytime."

"Why didn't you?"

He went silent, sullen. The way he contracted into himself was almost insect-like. Since I had been thinking of him as a rat in a cage, that's just how he was beginning to appear. His body looked thin and scrawny, his nose and chin pointy, greasy bristles of his beard became whiskers, his intense eyes like a rodent's peering from inside a sewer, his mouth full of pointy yellow teeth. I didn't know how much of it was my imagination, but once I viewed him this way it became impossible not to make the comparison.

Ignoring my question, he changed the subject. "Why are you here, Roger? Do you have no respect for the dying? Do you insist on harassing me? Let me die in peace."

"Not before you tell me what I want to know. For Christ's sake, James, can't you see what's happened to you? You used to be so strong, so healthy and happy. I used to look up to you, man. I really did."

He chuckled. "Yeah well, everything changes, nothing is fixed. You should know that. You with all your occult bullshit. Things change, time is mutable, and we ignorant humans get trapped in the past. That's what *it* is all about. That's why it came. It moves things forward, out of the past into the present. You might have looked up to me once, Roger. We might have been friends, too, and we were both even married once... but now that's all over. The time has come to bury the past."

He shrank even smaller, tightening the sheet around his waist, curling into a fetal position. He looked like a baby: sick, soiled, deranged, feral.

"I want to know what happened," I said. "And I'm tired of playing your games. I get it, all right. You're not going to scare me with your supernatural crapola. I'm starting to remember and the more I remember the more I accept this change in my reality. I've always known that there is more to earthly existence than what we experience. I've known it since I was a teenager. But I forgot that I knew it.

"So your parlor tricks won't work. I'm telling you this now, and I'm telling that thing in there with you. The Time Eater. You're gonna have to deal with me straight. Jesus, it's been at least sixteen years since I last saw you. You were that guy I wanted to be—confident, carefree, social, happy. Even after Jenny left me, and I was miserable and alone, I always knew you were the okay one, out there somewhere doing your thing. Somehow that made life bearable. Now look at you, man. Do you want to die?"

"No." His voice was small, petulant. "This isn't what I want. They told me I have no time left, that I'd be dead in less than a month. I came in too late, they said."

"You believe them? You take their word? You lay down and die?"

Silence. He was thinking. He had stopped looking like a rat. Now he looked like a child.

"The old James—the one I remember from Ohio State—wouldn't be put down like some sick dog. He would fight."

"But our past," he whispered, "is dead."

"Bullshit. You're lazy, you're depressed, and you want to die. You can't fool me, James. I'm the most depressed and bitter bastard on the planet, at least I was until I met Annabelle. Now you tell me what happened."

He exhaled a deep, weary breath. "Fine. I'll tell you about Celeste."

"I had the feeling it was about her," I said. "Start at the beginning."

He nodded. "It began that night, didn't it? I'm not going to sit here, blame you, lay a guilt trip on you, because I followed you into that darkness. I was a willing sacrifice. Shit, Roger, why do you think we were friends all those years? We had nothing in common. You don't realize that I actually looked up to you."

"Did you? No way. Yours was the picture perfect life—a sports scholarship, money. You were physically fit and attractive, popular with girls. You got invited to all the parties. You could snap your fingers and get whatever you wanted."

"I envied you. There was something about you… all that stuff you were into. It intrigued me. I know it seemed like everything always worked out for me, like there was never a problem, but in reality I knew that that right there—*in and of itself*—was a problem."

I chuckled. He asked why. "Because at least you were aware of it. That shows signs of intelligence. The fact that you suspected something was wrong not to have anything wrong shows you aren't a complete idiot."

"Thanks, I think," he said. "Then there was you. Man, you were fucked up. Nothing ever went your way, huh? People made fun of you. You couldn't get a date. I remember the first time I met you, I thought, *God, what's wrong with him?*"

I could only shake my head.

"But it was a good thing. I was attracted to it. You were the opposite of me, and you were far more real than everyone else. I wanted to know *why*."

"You mean, you didn't hang out with me because of my great personality?"

"The more time we spent together the better I liked you. Eventually we got to be best friends. But I was aloof, I know it; I won't apologize. You freaked me out, man. I had regular social activities I wasn't willing to give up: sports, girls, parties. I wasn't willing to give you up, either. I watched from a distance. Feigned ignorance. When you started casting spells, I feigned ignorance harder. It's a game: to pretend that you're stupid. People play it all the time. It can give you the upper hand."

"But I knew you knew!" I exclaimed. "Whenever I tried talking to you about my occult interests, you waved me off and told me I was acting crazy, but I would think, *He knows and he won't admit it.*"

"Yeah, so we both knew. I still didn't want to talk about it. Talking about it screwed up my partying life because I couldn't imagine both realities existing at once. Only one was allowed to be real. So I chose the party.

"But I watched. I paid attention. I analyzed everything you told me, all the weird shit that I witnessed while we were roommates, the people who started coming to see you asking for help. I thought it was strange, and I couldn't take it seriously. I'd say to myself, *Roger is only into that stuff because he can't get a girlfriend.*"

"You used to tell me that."

"That's right, I did. On the one hand, I believed it, but on the other, I suspected that what you were up to was more real than any of my social escapades."

"Nice to know that after I spent all those years feeling like a freak, like nobody understood me. I felt isolated, James. I was happy we were friends, I looked up to you, but I knew you didn't like me. I was a pity friend, the one who'd do your homework for you, and who you fell back on when everyone was busy."

He shook his head. "All true, guilty as charged, but I'm telling you that I also looked up to you, pal. My life was superficial. I was scared to live it any other way."

We sat in silence, in the swirling dark, and I gazed into the distance toward the dim, rolling planets and soaring, starry lights. The orb above James's head pulsed. The house in Brooklyn, with Annabelle sleeping soundly in her bed, seemed very far away.

"So you did come that night, all on your own," I said, suddenly understanding. "It was your chance to experience something *real.*"

He nodded, almost sheepishly.

I felt ready to move on. "Okay I got it, now tell me about everything you experienced *after* that night. Tell me about Celeste."

Her name seemed to produce a sound in the room, a rustling of leaves in wind. I felt the hair on the back of my neck stand up. I half expected her to come shambling out of the darkness like a fiend.

James's face had gone ashen. I could hardly believe it. James, lying there, was clenching his fists so tightly that blood was trickling down his wrists. He uttered a single word, expelling it with a rancid breath, *"Bitch."*

Again the rustling leaves. And then a gust of wind swept over us, fluttering the blankets on the bed. The darkness intensified, sucking the last of the color out of the room.

He grinned. "It's here."

"What is?"

"The Time Eater. It gets into everything, you know: the walls, the floor, the bed, the chair. It's in you, the same as it's in me. There is no escaping."

My fear level was rising, but I determined to get through this conversation without it turning into a metaphysical freak show.

"Celeste, James."

"But it's here. Eavesdropping."

"I don't care. I have to know."

He sat up straighter, losing his childlike quality and recovering his adult bearings. I found it strange how he could morph into so many incarnations right before my eyes.

"It's funny," he said. "That night galvanized me into getting serious about Celeste. She and I were dating, but it was mostly partying and sex, and I had been totally satisfied with that. But after our experience with the Time Eater, I realized how terrified I was, and I wanted to hide. I wanted to return to the world as it had been—before the sky cracked apart and madness leaked through—back to the comfortable things, like school, sports, and girls. Those things made up my world, not some beast in the sky, not some thing lurking beyond the veil. So I ignored it, refused it, and jumped headlong into a world of normalcy and safety. In short, I got married."

His last statement made me laugh. He looked at me confused. "What's so funny?"

"That you equate marriage with normalcy and safety. For me, it's the opposite. For me, marriage was harrowing, insane, unspeakable. I couldn't imagine getting married while I was in college, but when you moved out and got serious with Celeste, I followed in your footsteps. Although my marriage was anything but normal."

"That's because you married Jenny Morgan. Everybody knew she was nuts. I remember hearing stories of her bringing guys home from the bar, but instead of having sex with them she played twisted mind games with them. Do you know how crazy that sounds?"

"She was serious about her career."

"She was seriously nuts. When you two hooked up, I thought you were perfect for each other." He laughed bitterly. "I wanted nothing to do with it. The amount of weirdness generated by you two was not something I wanted in my life."

"You stopped associating with me."

"I did."

"You moved out and wouldn't answer my calls. You ignored me around campus. You stopped going to the bars we frequented. I blamed Celeste."

He stayed quiet.

"I had an idea, I suppose, that you were scared, that our experience that night drove us apart. You wouldn't even talk about it. I hated you for that. It made me realize I couldn't have real relationships doing what I was doing. No matter how many people I helped, there were twice as many I freaked out. If I did want to join society, I couldn't be involved with the occult, because it only enabled my alienation. So I gave it up. I stopped going to the library, the bookstores, stopped taking people's calls. I burned my papers, sold my items, trashed the rest, found a new place to live. I did the same thing as you, but for different reasons. I escaped reality. With Jenny."

James smiled. "It's like we pulled out of each other into these women, isn't it? Crazy. And away with these women we went, never to speak again. Until now."

"And now, again, we're alone."

He opened his mouth to respond, then closed it. I could see sadness in his eyes. He hated being alone as much as I did.

Lifting his head, his eyes brightened. He had a sudden recollection, saying, "It was wonderful at first. Celeste and I found what we were looking for in each other. I wanted escape into a normal life, and she wanted to marry the big man on campus.

"Back then, she had all these funky interests like poetry and art, but she was no artist. She was only trying to find herself. When she decided to double major in English and Education, not Performance Art Studies, I told her it was the right thing to do. She liked kids, so I suggested she teach K through 5. She went with that. In turn, she persuaded me that sports was not a real future and helped me get involved in computer science. We were the perfect American couple."

"So what happened?"

"Time passed. Routine set in. She found out she couldn't have children. The days started to get really, really long. We were happy because we had each other. Maybe it was good Celeste couldn't have children because it allowed us to focus on our careers. But then the trouble began."

He inhaled long and deep, his thin frame expanding with breath. I could imagine him shattering like a mirror dashed onto the floor, thousands of shards scattering, each containing a piece of James.

"When she stopped having sex with me, I just didn't get it, you know? Sex had been our strongest connection. We had no children, no adventurous dating life, and so we lacked the inherent spark that united us in the beginning. We had been married five years. What do people do in that situation?"

I shook my head, not really knowing what a couple would do.

"I'll tell you what we *had* been doing," he said. "Fucking. All the time, like bunnies, and I don't think we stopped fucking until Celeste stopped for good. Sex was our thing. We relied on it to get us through the bad times, and we did it to celebrate the good times. In the morning, once at night, sometimes in the afternoon, day after day after day—"

"I get it, you had a lot of sex." I felt annoyed, but didn't know why. I suspected it had something to do with the amount of sex Jenny and I had during our marriage, which, from the sound of it, was considerably less.

James shook his head. "No, we didn't just have a lot of sex. You're not getting it. We had a freakishly obsessive amount of sex. On the rare occasions when a day passed without us having sex, it was like an earthquake tremor had rumbled our foundations. It left us both feeling sad and confused. I would brood in anger, thinking in my head that she was a cold, frigid woman, a tease. I would imagine smashing her face with dinner plates as she washed the dishes."

"Jesus. You're sick," I said.

"Oh it gets worse. When a day passed without sex, Celeste would turn introspective and self-hating. She would think that I didn't love her, that I was having an affair, or that she was just a worthless human being no one could love. She'd cry, withdraw, appear wounded. This is when we had our really bad fights. In retrospect, I think we might've caused those fights simply so we could have makeup sex. After that, everything felt better. Except it wasn't. At that point, it was like fear kept us having sex, because we knew to stop was to invite the darkness, and so it was a race—a sex race—to outrun the bad feelings."

I thought, *Jenny and I talked about this. She said a lot of couples who were caught in a similar cycle came to her for therapy.*

James was looking me. "What are you thinking? Do you think it sounds crazy—the sex thing, I mean?"

"Of course it sounds crazy. But it's not that uncommon. Jenny told me stories about her patients—couples—who did that."

"She did?"

I nodded.

He considered a moment then said, "That makes me feel about this much better." He held up two fingers an inch apart.

"When did Celeste stop having sex with you?"

"I already told you, five years into the marriage. I came into the house after work one day and she was there on the couch, turned to the window, curtains open. It was summer and so the trees were bright and full, leaves ripe with color. She was just staring at them, like a zombie.

" 'Hey, aren't you gonna ask me about my day?' Yeah, I think that's what I said. She had always asked about my day when I came home. But that day she just stared out the window.

"I approached her angrily, was gonna grab her shoulders, whip her around, and demand that she say something. But when I got within a foot of her, she looked up. She had been crying. Bags under her eyes, mascara down her cheeks. In a tired, weak voice she said, 'I'm not going to let you rape me anymore,' and that's when I noticed the blood. There was some on the sofa, on her arm, her jeans. In one hand she held a small knife encrusted with blood. Her arm was slashed and gouged with a particularly nasty cut along her bicep.

"With a shock of horror, I realized she'd been cutting on herself. I once watched a documentary about cutters; usually they're teenage girls who come from terrible parents. Most had been sexually abused. But this wasn't some sickly teenage girl bleeding all over the sofa. It was my fucking wife."

The darkness in the room intensified, the orb over James's head fizzling out completely. I could barely see him now. A ghostly wind swirled between us.

I said, "That's really horrible, man. I'm sorry." And I meant it.

"There'd been signs, but I blocked them out. Celeste had taken on a gloomy disposition, especially around sex. She'd just roll over and sigh and then we'd fuck like that, not facing each other. A couple of times she'd told me no, but I didn't listen because I was trying to outrun the darkness. You understand."

I wasn't sure I did. Whenever Jenny and I had sex and she asked me to stop, which was frequently because she often experienced memories of her father molesting her, I stopped. I never pushed it.

"I'd been seeing bloodied tissues around," James went on, "but I assumed they were from her period. Instead, they were from her cutting and I just put the pieces together a little too late. It all came crashing down that day I found her on the sofa."

"What'd you do?"

"After adjusting to the shock, I swept her up and carried her to the car and then drove us to the emergency room. When the nurse asked me what happened, I had to tell the truth, that my wife had cut herself. 'Had she ever tried to commit suicide?' they wanted to know. I about broke into tears at the question. 'No,' I told them, firmly. 'She never had.' They put Celeste on suicide watch even though her wounds were superficial. I spent the night in the hospital waiting room."

I was startled by a gust of air pressing against my face, and I turned to find two glowing eyes in the dark.

Celeste, I thought. *She's come to listen.*

James spoke in a low, grave voice. "When she was released the next day, bandages up and down her arms, I was very angry that she had done this to herself, humiliated us, and kept me at the hospital. I got her home but she refused to talk. She stayed like that for days. I didn't know what to do. I still had to go to work, get the bills paid. Celeste took an extended leave from teaching. One day I came home while she was talking with her insurance. After she hung up, she turned to me and said, 'We are seeing Dr. Stetson on Monday.' Those words kick-started almost three years of marriage counseling."

The eyes crept closer, like a cat stalking its prey at night. I wasn't sure James noticed, but I wasn't about to say anything. I kept watch in case she decided to attack.

James recounted his therapy sessions, his struggle to get in touch with his emotions. He and Celeste sat in Dr. Stetson's office, talked about everything from sex to their childhoods, all in an effort to get at the root of the problem. Meanwhile, Celeste refused to have sex and started sleeping in a separate bed.

"We would've fought more if Celeste wasn't so withdrawn," he said. "She hardly spoke to me outside the therapy sessions. When she did, it was like talking to a robot. Drove me crazy."

"This lasted three years?"

"Just about. The marriage fell apart the day I came into Dr. Stetson's office and found Celeste and her new lover."

The glowing eyes inched closer.

"New lover? Holy shit, who was he? You make her sound sexually dysfunctional."

"She was. Except for that robot she could turn on. That's how she went back into teaching, by turning on her robot. Dr. Stetson even encouraged her, said it was a proper defense mechanism. It was the robot who had attracted this new lover, some snot-nosed kid."

Even closer.

"This the guy she left you for?"

James nodded. "Almost immediately after they hooked up, she moved out, got her own place and Chris moved in with her. A month later she filed for divorce."

"Didn't waste time. Got to appreciate that. Jenny dragged it out for almost a year. It was emotionally draining."

Closer.

"The part that was most infuriating was how Dr. Stetson goaded her, even encouraged her to divorce me and move in with Chris. 'She needs to free herself of your oppressiveness,' he told me. 'At this point,' he said, 'Celeste has got to do what's best for Celeste. There's been too much irreparable damage.' Can you believe that? What a bunch of shit. 'What about me?' I asked him. 'What the hell am I supposed to do?' You know what he said?"

"What?"

Closer.

"I needed to take some time to get to know myself. He said I was a monster and I didn't realize it. I was totally out of touch with my emotions and was hurting people. She cheats on me and leaves me for some punk kid and *I'm* the monster. Of course her and that kid didn't last too long. She slept around after that; eventually she got married again to some rich doctor with two kids—"

Celeste suddenly sprang out of the dark, flying through the air like a tiger, claws raised, teeth gnashing. She landed with a crash, smashing into James and knocking him off the mattress. It was so dark that I could hardly tell what was happening; they seemed to be careening about in the black gulf opposite the bed.

I tried to leap up from my chair to help, but something invisible restrained me.

"What the hell?" I cried.

The shadows in the room were now so intense they appeared tangible. Stars in the distance flared; planets and satellites rolled vigorously. A front of nebulous space dust moved in, providing distorted visibility.

Then, *suction.*

It's here in the room with us, I thought.

A strong wind pulled me; my clothes, my hair, my skin—yanked so violently I thought I would be flayed alive. The bedclothes stripped off, leaving only the mattress. Stars and planets began gliding toward the left.

I became aware of a barely audible hum, a low-frequency vibration rattling in my ears. I could sense the thing in my periphery. The Time Eater. Sense it more than see it. Vast black spot darker than the surrounding darkness, within which there was nothing, void. The outer edges of it flickered. From my perspective, it resembled a colossal amoeba floating in space.

I searched for James and Celeste as I struggled to free myself, but there was no sign of them. The suction created a hollowness in my stomach that felt like my insides were being torn out. I gritted my teeth, writhing in a war against some unseen entity, crushed under the weight of that thunderous hum. I could not think or draw breath.

I'm going die in this chair. It's going to swallow me, absorb me, digest my soul, grind up my body with the past and spit bones back. God help me...

James reemerged, clambering onto the mattress, clutching it to resist the wind. His face was a grimace of pain, and a trickle of blood stained his chin. The suction ripped at his clothes, pulling his hair.

"NO," he was shouting, "NO! NO! NO!" and then he slipped into an unintelligible scream.

Withered arms groped up from the black behind the bed. Curled into claws, they wrapped around James's shoulder and neck, hoisting Celeste onto the mattress like a snake out of its hole. She appeared unaffected by the tremendous suction, her lizard-like body lead, an iron weight that scrambled on top of James and held him there, pinning his limbs.

The Time Eater pulled, but none of us budged. We were all fastened in place by magic beyond our knowing. The stars, satellites, and planets, not so fortunate, were slowly drawn out of space and sucked into that vast wriggling amoeba full of darkness, which seemed to linger at the edge of my periphery, just out of sight.

I'm seeing behind *reality,* I thought. *I'm seeing behind everything, behind the illusion of time.*

And then a follow-up thought: *And there, the beast dwelleth…*

But *was* it truly a beast? Could I be sure? What if it was God, the being responsible for creating the universe, sending down its substance in the guise of Moses, Jesus, Shakyamuni, and Mohammed? What if such a being was nothing more than a trundling, churning mass, sweeping over everything, endlessly destroying and recreating?

The thought sent shivers down my spine.

To my surprise, James's screams morphed into the rudiments of words, phrases, syllables. Most astonishing was when he called, "I want to live! I do—I want to live!" over and over. I almost broke into tears for him.

"Hell yeah!" I shouted, struggling again to get free of the chair. "That's the James I remember!"

My voice seemed to encourage him because he glanced about, pain becoming recognition in his face. When he saw me he grinned. "You wanted the old James? You got him!" he said, and quite brutally and suddenly whipped an elbow around his head, striking Celeste in the eye.

"Holy shit!" I screamed.

The shrieking, writhing female form who should not be tumbled off James onto her back, clutching her face. Blood seeped through her fingers. The wind pulled at James's clothes as he straddled her, a look of rage in his eyes as he landed blow after blow on her soft undead flesh.

Gradually she was mashed into a bloody pulp, a fizzling red puddle that turned to black and shrank down, liquefying, until Celeste ceased to be. The wind abruptly stopped. James was left kneeling in the muck, his pajama bottoms bloodstained, as the shadows lessened, allowing the soft glow of overhead light to return to the room.

My restraints evaporated and I leaped to my feet. As I stood beside the bed, looking at James, I became aware of the Time Eater slithering back behind the veil of reality, back where it belonged. With its presence gone everything felt heavy with substance. I drew a syrupy breath.

James held out his hands doused in foulness and blood. His face was red, his mouth a scowl, his eyes full of intensity. I couldn't tell what he was thinking. But I remembered his triumphant *I want to live!* And that, it seemed, was the most important thing. That was going to change everything.

"You okay?" I said.

He'd gone still, his body rigid as a cemetery statue, while beneath him the puddle that was Celeste dissolved. All trace of her had vanished from his arms, his hands, his pajama bottoms. Soon she was gone completely, wiped away, only a figment of our imaginations.

"Oh God..." James wailed, collapsing on the bed into a blubbering mess. "I killed her, I killed her! She's gone..."

I sat down, stroking his back. His body was hot to the touch and as rough as sandalwood. He went fetal like a baby, bawling, hands over his face.

"I killed her... God... I killed Mommy!"

My ears pricked up at the word: *Mommy*. Had he just said *I killed Mommy?*

"Hey man, it's all right. You didn't do anything."

He didn't hear me, just kept shivering, sobbing, curling into a tighter position. *He's trying to shrink himself,* I thought. *He wants to disappear.*

"Come on. Let's get you covered up." I searched around the bed until I located one of the blankets and a pillow. I draped him with the former, positioning the latter under his head. He still refused to look at me.

I continued stroking his back, hoping to calm him. Overhead, the light swelled to life and the bedroom became brightly visible. The planets and stars winked out—except for those hovering outside the window, clear in the night sky.

The Time Eater is gone, I thought, with no small amount of relief. *At least for now...*

James wouldn't talk to me no matter what I did, and eventually he fell asleep. His snores reverberated in the room. The boxes and piled old clothes loomed around us like penitent monks, offering their prayers to the sick, the lame, my friend James from college who'd somehow been turned into... *this.*

I killed her, I killed mommy. His last words buzzed through my head. I sighed with heaviness, feeling the weight of the situation pressing on me. I was certain I'd acquired another few pieces of the puzzle, but my brain was not functional enough to connect them. I needed sleep.

After making sure he was tucked in, I got up and headed for the door. He muttered something and I wheeled, his voice startling me.

"What's that, James?"

He shifted on the mattress. "Moh... mor... morphine."

The word stung the air. I recalled the image of him on the bed, arms outspread and riddled with dangling syringes. It gave me a dreadful fright.

I crossed to the door, switched off the light, and let myself out into the hall. For a second, I felt like I was falling down a long, bottomless shaft.

Chapter Twelve

My head ached from the alcohol I had consumed the night before. Annabelle's soft body lay next to me. I touched her, testing its realness. She stirred.

"What time is it?" she asked.

I glanced at the alarm clock. "Almost eleven."

"Shit."

"What?"

"Norma will be here."

I had forgotten about the pretty nurse with the crystal blue eyes. My intuition told me she knew more than any regular nurse should know about James's condition. I would have to investigate.

"What's the problem with Norma?" I asked.

Annabelle propped herself on one elbow. "Are you kidding? She's a potential murder victim. Whatever is inside James is looking to kill her just as it killed those other girls, Celeste and…"

"—Jenny, my ex-wife, thank you. I'm not sure James actually killed them. I mean, I'm pretty sure he ended their existence. But murder? No, I don't think he did that."

Disbelief entered her eyes. "How do you explain yesterday? He must have snuck out, kidnapped them, killed them, and now he's reanimating them, using that voodoo crap you were telling me about."

"It's more complicated than that, Annabelle."

She glared at me. For the first time I thought I saw hatred there. The hatred that two people experience toward each other after long periods of exposure: marriage hatred, roommate hatred, or parental hatred. Luckily, it didn't linger long.

She sighed, shrugged, flipping her hair over her shoulder. "Of course," she said. "What do I know about any of this? You two are the occultists."

I noticed the flash of resentment aimed unconsciously at me for not letting her explain away these events with murder. Resentment that remained, festering, darkening.

We'll have to deal with that eventually, I thought.

I tried ignoring all of the psychological inferences my brain was making about the situation. I focused on the moment, the *now*, letting my eyes wander over the wonderland of Annabelle's body. She had on a white tank top so thin I could see the swell of her nipples. Her milky smooth neck, her chin, red mouth, angular nose, and gorgeous eyes. The endless ebony spilling down her shoulders in waves. She caught me looking.

Chuckling, she said, "Did you remember something important?"

"Yeah. I'm in bed with a beautiful woman."

"Oh? Why not do something about it?"

I grinned, "Maybe I will," and leaned in for a kiss.

She met me halfway, our tongues careening like two ships in a storm. I felt the warmth of the sun inching across the bed. We had been kissing for five minutes when the door slammed downstairs.

Annabelle stopped. "Shit, Norma." She jumped out of the bed, starting to get dressed. I followed her.

She finished before me and headed out into the hall. For some reason I lingered, looking around Annabelle's distinctly feminine room. Slipping my shirt on, I walked over to the dresser with the large mirror surmounting it. On the wood surface was an array of makeup products and jewelry. I imagined Annabelle sitting there, combing her long black hair in the mirror, thinking to herself, humming. The loneliness of the image made me sad.

I heard voices downstairs and hurried to finish getting dressed. I happened to glance at a photograph pinned to the wall by the door. It was like something old and forgotten, pinned there since who knows when, unframed, corners curling in.

It showed a younger, less somber version of Annabelle wearing hospital scrubs and a red headband. Her hair, black as ever, was only shoulder length. Her skin had more color and she wore an expression of excitement and hope, almost naiveté.

That's gotta be from seven or eight years ago, I thought. *And that's gotta be her ex-husband, the doctor. Jon.*

Standing beside her in the photograph was a lean, attractive man who reminded me of an actor in a soap opera. He had a chiseled face, short brown hair, with eyes that oozed confidence, arrogance, and narcissism. I laughed when I realized he resembled a young James.

There's the guy I never got to be. The popular guy in high school, the head of a fraternity in college. Gets all the women in the world, then shrugs them off like he deserved them anyway.

The photograph stirred up my bitter feelings. Seeing Annabelle's ex-husband sent me into a fit of jealousy, as I remembered the stories she had told me about him. I wished him dead. I wished some psychotic lover went berserk after discovering he was cheating on her and cut his balls off.

I headed downstairs.

Norma and Annabelle were in the kitchen, sitting at the table having coffee. The nurse in her blue scrubs shot me back into the photograph upstairs. When I looked at Annabelle I saw her whole life flash before my eyes on fast-forward.

I could tell she hadn't told Norma anything. Her jaw was clenched, her body rigid. She seemed on the verge of exploding.

"Look, it's Mr. Borough," Norma said. I was surprised she remembered my last name.

"Good morning," I replied.

She pulled out the chair beside her. "Sit over here by me. Annabelle was just about to tell me something important, she says."

I sat down. Annabelle caught my attention with her eyes and held it. She looked terrified.

I nodded slightly, enough so she could see but not enough to tip off Norma, signaling that I would do it if she wanted me to. I had no problem serving as a beans-spiller. At this point in the game, I didn't have much to lose.

"You two are acting funny," Norma said, eyeing us in a semi-cross manner. Then, to Annabelle, hooking a finger toward me: "You found out he's married, didn't you?"

Annabelle erupted with laughter. As she did all signs of tension drained from her face. It was as if a cleansing wave passed over her. "I *wish* it was something that simple," she said. "At least then I'd have an idea what to do."

Norma scrunched her eyebrows. Even wearing an expression of confusion, I noticed how clear and discerning her blue eyes were. She was younger, yes, and attractive, yes, but there was an aura of age surrounding her too. No, not age: experience. No not even that: *wisdom*. But it was a sinister kind of wisdom. Yes, I could see that now, although at first it had been hidden. *She knows more than she's letting on.*

"Is it something about James?" she asked, and suddenly her face tightened. "Oh God, he passed already?"

"No, nothing like that," I said, grabbing the reins. "He's hanging in there, but he's getting worse."

She nodded. "'Course he is. He's dying, isn't he? Doc Sanderson says he'll be lucky to finish the week."

I cringed at this, disliking the fatalism of her statement. I glanced at Annabelle, wondering how to proceed, but she gave me a blank expression. I decided to go for it.

"We've discovered something about James's condition."

Eyebrows lifted. "You have, have you? I didn't realize you were a doctor, Mr. Borough."

"I'm not. Annabelle was a nurse, though. But this is different. It has nothing to do with doctors or medicine. And Norma, I'm going to have to ask you to keep an open mind about this. Can you do that?"

"Depends. I'm under the employment of the hospital. I have to report everything back to them. I have the patient's best interest in mind, so if you tell me something I think compromises his interests, well…"

I'd expected she'd say this. And I had a counter ready. "Do you attend church, Norma?"

"Every Sunday."

"So you believe in God?"

"'Course I do. I just said I attend church every Sunday."

"That's good because what I'm about to tell you falls under the heading of spirituality. In my opinion, James's spirit is sick. That's why he's dying, not because of some inoperable brain tumor. His soul is under attack by a demon. This demon has possessed him."

She looked from me to Annabelle, then back to me. I noticed how tense she suddenly got. Her spine straightened, jaws narrowed. Her stare became a fixed beam emanating from her face.

"How do you feel about what I just said?" I asked.

"Well, I believe in the devil, Mr. Borough. And, sure, Pastor Serius sometimes makes his references about demons and folks being possessed. But to be honest, I've never experienced it firsthand. I've just seen some of those ridiculous horror movies about demons and frankly, I think they're rubbish."

"You do?"

She nodded. "I'm a certified nurse, Mr. Borough. I have been at this profession going on nine years. That is to say, I've seen a lot. But none of it has anything to do with demons. Folks get sick. Folks see a doctor and get treated. Sometimes they get better; a lot of times they don't. But really, I can't believe demons got anything to do with it."

"I've seen it," Annabelle said, sounding desperate. "Yesterday, while I was working. James's voice called me into his room. I went to check on him and found... Christ, I don't know what I found. Something is terribly wrong with him. He looked deranged, evil."

"Folks can get like that when they're dying."

Annabelle shook her head. "No, this was different. I've never seen anything like it. There was something in the room with him, something dark and terrible. It covered everything in its shadow."

I watched Norma's face rumple, saw skepticism enter her eyes—that and annoyance and *hate*. She wasn't believing a word Annabelle said.

"Just what are you tellin' me?" she asked.

"That James wasn't alone. *Things* were in there with him. Two of them came out of the dark, tied me to the chair, gagged me."

"Say what?"

"One of them was his ex-wife, Celeste, the girl who's gone missing. I think James may have killed her while he was possessed by the demon."

Norma slammed her hand down on the table, hard, making us both jump. "That's enough," she said. "I don't want to hear any more about it. I don't appreciate being made a fool of."

"Nobody thinks you're a fool," I said.

But she held her hand up at me. "I am a God-fearing Christian, but I am also a nurse, and I have a job to do. People get sick because of bacteria, viruses, and bad genes, not because of demons. If you wanted to play a practical joke, then congratulations because you've succeeded."

"It's nothing like that, Norma," Annabelle said, starting to cry. "I swear we're telling the truth."

Norma *mm-hmm*ed, then got up from the chair, clutching her bag. "Very good acting, dear, but the joke's over. If you'll excuse me, I have a patient to treat." She turned her back, heading for the stairs.

Something's not right here, I thought. *She's supposed to listen, understand, help us. I was sure she knew more about this but it's clear she's as scared as the rest of us. She could get hurt up there.*

I lunged from my seat, stood before the stairs, blocking her. She looked startled, frightened—furious.

"We won't be requiring your services anymore, Norma," I said.

"That isn't up to you, Mr. Borough. The hospital has assigned me to James, and if you prevent me from seeing him I'll have no choice but to report back to Doc Sanderson and the other doctors. If I tell them about this demon business, they're likely to find you unfit to care for James. They'll come and take him back to the hospital. Is that what you want?"

"Of course not. But we're telling the truth. James is under attack."

She raised her medical bag. "You're right, he is under attack. From withdrawals. He should have had his morphine shot before eleven."

For some reason, the mention of morphine set my blood boiling. All I could think about was the crucifixion image James had showed me, his arms a pincushion of hypodermic needles. I was sure James— the real James—had been trying to tell me something.

"He doesn't need narcotics," I said.

She chuckled. "Narcotics? The morphine keeps him out of pain. You want him to suffer, that it? How about bathing him, helping him to the bathroom. You gonna do that?"

"As a matter of fact, I am."

She scoffed and tried to pass but I refused to let her up the stairs. "Good day to you, Norma," I said.

She had been looking at my feet, but now her head lifted, ever so slowly, and as she did a shadow passed over the room, darkening it. She glared at me, eyes turning black, and instead of pupils she had mini solar systems, sockets full of darkness, planets, and stars.

Suddenly I understood. *It's got her under its spell, controlling her thoughts and actions like it controls James's thoughts and actions. For how long? Always? Just this morning?*

My brain began whirring, spinning, puzzling it all out. I realized she had probably been doing its bidding this whole time, keeping James deranged and weak by pumping him full of morphine. James's proclamation of *I want to live* made more sense to me. Smothered as he was beneath a blanket of dope and darkness, he was desperately trying to break out.

The first step was getting him off the drugs and away from this Time Eater henchwoman.

She let out a scream that vibrated the picture frames on the wall and came at me, claws to my face. Her mouth, now swinging down unnaturally and displaying pointy stars for teeth, emit a stream of canine drool. The sight of her flickering with darkness froze me in place. I failed to evade her attacks, and she crashed into me, teeth and nails tearing, wailing an awful cry.

I shouted as pain pierced my flesh. Norma's exaggerated mouth came closing down around the front of my skull. My eyes beheld the deep, dark vision of her soul, an endless void, a sea of emptiness in which stars burned, planets rolled, and meteors streamed like falling embers.

Faces appeared in the black and scowled at me; some of them wore cone-shaped white cloth hats and swung nooses overhead like lassos. I felt myself being pulled into some forgotten nether place, a place from where I might never emerge again.

Just as the vision overwhelmed me, a tremendous impact shook the fabric of my reality. The world vibrated like a tuning fork. Stars and planets veered off course to go crashing into the black sea. The hateful faces shouted, then slowly dissolved and dispersed, until at last a ray of light spilt the mold, guiding out, away, to freedom.

I blinked, looked up, and saw Annabelle crouching over me. In one quivering hand she held a baking pin. Her face was a mess of terror and shock. She whispered to me, "Is it, did it… is she gone? I hit—" and then it became too much and she dropped the baking pin and collapsed to her knees, weeping.

In a daze I got to my feet, body aching. I noticed with a grunt of disgust that my front was covered in a slimy brackish liquid. When I tried wiping it from my clothes it evaporated into thin air. A moment later, I was no longer covered in it.

I stood beside Annabelle and placed a hand on her shoulder. Strands of black hair spilled between my fingers. She was sobbing, holding her face. I did my best to console her.

"I smashed her," she said, somewhere between shock and amazement. "I took the baking pin out of the cupboard, crept behind her and let her have it! *God*—Norma!"

She burst into tears again, but I said, "You did the right thing, Annabelle. You saved my life."

Sniffling, she said, "I know. I did. But don't you understand? It felt horrible! I even liked her! But when I hit her I screamed in rage that I hated her, hated her so much, and all I felt inside was murderous rage. I probably killed her. Is she going to die? Oh god oh god oh god..."

"Come on. Everything is going to be all right."

"But I'm a bad person!" she said. "Evil, wicked! I didn't even know I could feel like that—"

I helped her off the floor and escorted her into the living room. For a moment, I glanced over my shoulder, wondering if any trace of the nurse remained, but the stairs were spotless and vacant. Norma had simply vanished.

There was a leather wraparound couch in front of the Plasma screen. Before it sat a glass table piled with *Reader's Digest* and various golfing magazines. I got her over to the couch, then opened the blinds, letting in the sun.

I sat next to her, leaned back, and she curled into my lap, bringing up her knees. She cried like a baby. I knew this was her big release. Everything had been building inside her and now she was full and had to let it out. My job was to be there while she did it.

"I don't know what I'm doing," she said finally, then chuckled. "I'm losing my mind. Is that it?"

My turn to chuckle. "If there's one thing I've learned since coming here, it's that we're all losing our minds."

She slugged my arm. "But is all this real?"

"None of it is real. Everything we *think* is real is just an illusion."

"That doesn't help."

"It's the truth. Trying to figure out what is and isn't real will ensure you actually do lose your mind. The best approach is to deal with it as it comes. That's what I've found."

She nodded, considering. "I suppose you're right. It's all so complicated, like I fell down the rabbit hole of Alice in Wonderland."

"The comparison is not far-off. Look, I have some experience with this. In college I lived primarily in a world where magic existed. It was little magic, play magic, and sure it worked but it never dismantled reality the way the Time Eater does. The Time Eater is more than magic; it's something else."

"What's the Time Eater?"

"The thing behind reality. The being James and I summoned that night at Ohio State."

"It eats time?"

"I'm not sure what it does with time. But in my mind, that's the only word I have for it. Anyway, it certainly does *something* to time. Mutates it, distorts it."

Annabelle was shaking her head. "I don't know. I'm glad you're here. I think I'd fall apart if you weren't."

I held her closer. "I'm not going anywhere. We're going to ride this out together and bring James back."

"We are?"

I nodded. "He said something last night. He said, 'I want to live,' just like that. We had been talking about Celeste, how the divorce had changed him, crippled him, left him in a place where he felt like dying."

"What about his tumor? The month to live and everything?"

"I believe he brought that on himself, that his misery was so great after Celeste left him that his body expressed his remorse as a tumor."

She scrunched her eyebrows. "I agree that a person's lifestyle can affect their health, but I used to be a nurse, Roger. I've never seen anything like what you're describing."

"That may be true. But please keep in mind that you've never seen a Time Eater before, either, and now you have."

"Touché."

"My point is that James's unbalanced condition brought on a terminal illness, and since he was so despondent about the divorce and where his life ended up afterward, he accepted his one month to live with open arms. He already wanted to die anyway. He dug himself a hole up there in the spare bedroom, got hooked on morphine, and waited for death. But only one problem: he didn't anticipate the return of the Time Eater. Now reality has been shunted, thrown off-course, and we're all spiraling into the unknown."

"So what do we do?"

"We contact this guy." I reached into my pocket and took out the business card Alexander had given me. I handed it to Annabelle, who turned it over, unconvinced.

"An acupuncturist?"

I nodded.

With a scoff, she said, "All that Oriental Medicine stuff is a joke."

"Is it?"

"Yes, it is. When Jon and I were together, we had this ongoing laugh about it. A lot of the girls who were nurses at the hospital were always running off to study so-called *Oriental Medicine*. They thought they wouldn't have to change bedpans or prescribe medication, that they could just stick needles in people and they'd get better. Jon thought it was the biggest scam ever."

"Do you think it's a scam?"

She chewed her bottom lip. "I did, especially with Jon. And the girls who went to study it usually came back to the hospital, tails between their legs. But honestly I don't really know how I feel about it. I know it isn't respected among Western doctors."

"All they respect is the narcotic and the knife."

"Oh come on, that's a little harsh." Her eyes strayed back to the business card. She read it aloud, the words lingering in the air. I could tell she was struggling to give it a chance. When she handed it back, she said, "At this point, I'll try anything."

"Good, because in order for this to work we've got to believe it will work."

"Explain that."

"How 'bout some coffee?"

We got up from the sofa and went into the kitchen. Annabelle brewed another pot of joe. We sat at the table, not speaking, waiting for the coffee to finish. After our mugs were filled, we got back to our conversation.

"I'm convinced this is all linked to James's impending death," I said. "He hated himself, he wanted to die, and so he got sick and the Time Eater showed up. Until now, he's been letting the being possess him at will, to work its madness through him. But last night, after I had a long talk with him, his attitude changed. He told me seriously that he wanted to live. This is the crucial point. If we can get James back into the realm of the living, the Time Eater should return from whence it came."

"And you think this funky acupuncturist can help?"

"I do, but only now that James has *decided* he wants to live. Only because he's shifted his intention. Now, we must shift ours."

"But of course I want James to live!" she said.

"I know. I'm asking you to imagine that it's *possible* for him to live. I want you to forget this one-month crap—and forget the rest of Western medicine, while you're at it. We're entering into a totally different zone. We have to remain open as we make the transition. Can you do it?"

She smiled and took my hand. "With you, I can do anything. But tell me, where did you get that business card?"

"I went to an occult bookstore in the city yesterday and told the owner the whole story."

"You did? When, with my car?"

I nodded.

"And he believed you?

More nodding. "When I told him about James, he gave me the card and told me to call the acupuncturist."

"So what are we waiting for?" She retrieved her phone from the countertop and gave it to me.

I dialed. After a few rings, a woman with a thick Chinese accent answered.

"Is this the office of Li Xi?" I asked.

A pause, then: "How you know dat?"

"I got his business card from Alexander at *Cosmos, Psyche, and Higher Worlds*. My friend has fallen ill and Alexander seemed to think Li Xi could help."

"Ah. OK. You come in one hour thirty minutes. The doctor will see you then. You come alone."

She rattled off an address in the city, which I repeated to Annabelle, who wrote it down on a paper towel. I hung up and said, "Looks like I'm going back into the city."

"Now?"

"That's what the woman said. I can see the doctor in an hour and a half."

"Can I go with you?"

"She said to come alone."

"Why? I don't want to stay by myself with James. Couldn't I wait in the car?"

"You could. But who knows how long this will take, it could be hours, and why risk it? She said to come alone, so I think I'd better do as she says."

"What will I do?"

I squeezed her hand. "Just stay out of his room and you'll be fine. No matter what, even if he calls for you and says he's dying, you stay out."

She nodded, eyes turned down. "I'll be safe as long as I stay out of there, huh?"

"That's right. Haven't you got some work you could do?"

"Piles of it. But it hardly seems relevant now."

"That's not true. When we make it through this, you'll still need to have clients and be able to pay your bills. Work might get your mind off things."

She brought my hand to her lips, kissed it. Despite all that had happened, the feeling sent a jolt of pleasure through me. I smiled at her, touching her face. The more time we spent together, the more I felt myself falling for her.

She got up and took the car keys off their little peg on the wall. "Do you think it needs gas?"

"Probably. I'll fill it up on the way."

She handed me the directions and I plugged them into my smartphone. Then she walked me to the door. The noon sun was rising high above the buildings. Trees lining the road swished in the wind.

"Promise you'll come back?" she said.

"I promise."

She leaned down for a kiss, then waved and vanished into the house. I got into the car and headed toward the skyscrapers in the distance.

Chapter Thirteen

I had been through Chinatown plenty of times, but usually on the way to somewhere else. It took me forever to find the right streets, even longer the right area, and even longer to park the car. By the time my feet touched the grimy cement, the sun was veering off toward the west.

The streets were congested with traffic: tourists, businessmen, shoppers. A healthy mixture of different Asian groups, with a smattering of whites and blacks thrown in. Cars and taxis plunged down the roadways, honking, flicking cigarette butts.

The shop fronts bustled with activity, and food was everywhere, little trinkets by the sidewalk, clothes and picture frames, bottles of herbs, key chains, glass display cases of jewelry. Music and bootleg DVDs, porn, smut animation, Buddhist pamphlets, chopsticks and Chinese bowls, a life-size cardboard cutout of Mao Zedong. After what felt like ages, I located the correct address and turned down an alley.

Instantly it got quieter, darker, smellier. Dumpsters flanked a potholed strip of asphalt, over which a stream of foul liquid coursed. I saw rats and roaches rummaging in the stacked trash bags.

You've got to be kidding me.

As I started walking, one of the doors banged open and a short, muscular Asian wearing a red and white headband plunged out. He was in the middle of shouting at someone, but when he saw me he stopped. He had a cigarette in the corner or his mouth, eyes like two round bolts. He puffed on the cigarette, hurling a bag of trash onto one of the piles. Insects and vermin scattered. He took another look and vanished back inside.

I started walking again. The farther I went down the alley, the darker and quieter it got, like I was leaving the city behind. A small red door at the end had the numbers I was looking for, along with a sign that said *Acupuncture*. I pressed the round buzzer and waited.

When the door swung open, my eyes gazed upon the most gorgeous Asian woman I had ever seen. She was short, thin, and pale, with long hair and mischievous eyes. She wore a loose-hanging silver top that left little to the imagination.

"Mr. Borough?" she said.

"Yes—"

Before I could ask how she knew my name, one of her tiny hands shot over the threshold and pulled me in. The door slammed closed with a resounding clang. I was standing in an office, walls lined with books and posters. Chinoiserie style lamps and fans hung from the ceiling; a bonsai tree in the corner of the room displayed its branches proudly; in the other corner, a miniature stone garden lay raked and silent. There was a child sitting in the garden. He was playing a handheld video game with the sound turned down.

The woman walked around behind the desk, giving me a nice showing of her long legs. When she was seated, she motioned for me to join her in one of the adjacent chairs.

Producing a folder, she began flipping through it. "It says here your friend very sick, gonna die soon."

"That's right. How do you..."

She waved a hand at me. I caught a whiff of nail polish. "I spoke to Alexander at the bookstore and he gave me whole story."

"Ah," I said.

After a while of flipping through the folder, she turned to the computer and punched keys. I was nervous; my hands sweated. She was so extremely attractive, I couldn't help but feel a little awkward.

"He'll want to meet you, examine you, before he do anything," she said.

"That's fine."

"After he meet you, he'll decide whether or not to come see your friend."

"It's an emergency."

She looked up from the screen to my face, studying me with her dark eyes. "If doctor feels it's necessary, he'll come."

"Even to Brooklyn?"

"Even to anywhere."

She went back to typing, and I set my mind at ease. I was sure he'd think it was important enough.

"He'll see you in a few minutes," she said. "Just sit and wait."

I nodded as she got up and rounded the desk, disappearing through the door on my left. I was alone for the next five minutes, just me and the kid who seemed totally oblivious to anything save his video game. She eventually stuck her head back out and said, "Doctor ready now." I got up and she led me into a long hall. I was weighed and then had to stick my tongue out while she studied it and jotted down notes. "This just formality," she said.

After that, I was brought to a large room divided into partitions by folding Chinese screens. I was installed on my back on a padded table and asked to wait. I could hear water trickling somewhere and New Age music from overhead speakers. It was a while before the doctor arrived. I began to doze.

The moment he entered, he stopped and stared at me with an unnerving expression. He was, quite honestly, exactly as I expected him to be: squat, solid, elderly, bearded, and gray-haired. Though short, his body was a rock; just looking at him, I doubted I'd be able to budge him an inch. His hair was deep and ashy, flowing down his back. Big bushy caterpillars slept on his forehead, and his eyes, dark and vastly penetrating, told of experience and wisdom.

"Hello," I mumbled, feeling dwarfed in his presence.

He kept silent, then stepped forward. His gaze softened and all at once he appeared kind and benevolent. Even his voice, while gruff, had a cheery air.

"Good to meet you, Mr. Borough," he said. "I'm Doctor Li Xi." He stuck his hand out and I shook; it felt like grabbing a tree trunk.

"Good to meet you too," I said. "Please, call me Roger."

He bowed slightly. "Yes, Roger. And you call me Dr. Li."

I nodded.

He came to where I lay on the padded table. The young Chinese girl followed, flitting about in his wake like a butterfly. I noticed she was absolutely silent in Dr. Li's presence, and much less mischievous, almost submissive. He had the folder in his hand, was flipping through it. "Lie back, please," he said.

"I think there's been a mistake. I'm not the one who's sick, it's my friend—"

"I know that much, it says so here in your folder, but please lie back anyway. If you've spent any time around your friend in the last forty-eight hours, then I can gauge his energy from you."

I didn't really know what that meant, but it sounded good and so I did as he said. Laying my head down, I closed my eyes, drifted away to the New Age music, and soon I felt his fingers being dragged up and down my body. Very lightly, the ghost of a touch. Every so often I'd hear him mutter something. When he was finished, he told me to sit up.

"Show me your tongue," he said.

I did, and he spent a few minutes studying it. Then he took my pulse three different times, in three different ways, and afterward he asked me to lie down again. He took the folder and left to confer with his assistant, assuring me he'd be right back.

It was not long. A moment later I was following the receptionist back out to the waiting room, where the little boy was playing his video game. She told me to wait for the doctor.

When Dr. Li reemerged, he was no longer wearing a white lab coat. He wore a tight gray suit, his coat slung over his arm, a leather doctor's bag and umbrella in one hand, a small overnight bag in the other. He gave me a funny look. "We go to Brooklyn, yes?"

I shot to my feet. "Um, yes—now? Yes—okay, good."

"I work for money. You do have money, right?"

I blanched. "Um—yes. Yes, we have money." I just hoped that, together, Annabelle and I could cover the cost.

He caught me staring at his overnight bag and said, "Just in case. Sometimes these things require that I stay by the patient several days. Is that a problem?"

"That won't be a problem."

He started for the door, then, chuckling, informed me, "Good, we go. You drive. I sleep."

Twenty minutes later, we were battling the traffic toward Brooklyn.

*   *   *

He did sleep. Almost the whole trip. I had thought he would question me and ask about James, what were his symptoms, that sort of thing, but the moment we got in the car he faced the window and began to snore. I drove aggressively, anxious to be back.

When I pulled into the driveway, the sun had descended over the western horizon. Dr. Li roused from sleep ten minutes earlier, but still he had said very little, and what he did say seemed trivial and unimportant. I kept looking for opportunities to talk about James, but before I found any we'd arrived.

I assisted Dr. Li and took his bags, leading him up the front steps. He was so calm and serene, with his small eyes, gray hair, and sleepy grin, that I was constantly reminded of my own discomfort and unease whenever he looked at me. He possessed that overall characteristic— to mirror back the darkness within a person. Randolf of *Randolf's Rare Books* had had a similar effect on people.

As I let him in the house, I was flooded by a deep sense of dread. It came from the house itself, from the walls, ceiling, and furniture, a slowly leeching darkness, and I realized at once the Time Eater knew we were here.

It must be upset. Good, let it be. This is payback.

The dread was sticking to me, oozing down and weighting my steps. Darkness gathered into my chest, forming a knot. It was a terrible feeling.

Dr. Li surprised me by saying, "You take that into you… that no good."

We were moving down the hall toward the kitchen. I stopped. "Take what into me?"

He gestured with his hands. "All this, all that is around, all that has converged here. Black spirits, emptiness. I watched you suck it into yourself when we came through the door. That no good, you must repel it—like this!" He shoved both hands, palms out, away from his chest, and made a *humph* noise.

"You try," he said. "You push the bad energy away using your will. Imagine you can even see it leaving you. That helps."

I did as he said, feeling a bit silly, but the moment I completed the action I felt lighter, less murky.

"It worked!" I said.

The doctor smiled. "Some very bad spirits in here. It will be a challenge to keep them out." He bowed slightly, signaling for me to lead the way, and we started for the kitchen.

"Annabelle?" I called, flipping on the light and setting down Dr. Li's bags. The harsh yellow mixed with the purple twilight from the window. "Annabelle?"

When she didn't answer, I panicked. *Don't tell me she went up into his room again...*

"Have you tea?" the doctor asked.

His request distracted me, which I realized was his intention. "Right, yes, tea," I said and put the kettle on, retrieving three mugs instead of two, hoping Annabelle would join us.

"Black tea, if you've got it," he added. "I need caffeine."

I fixed the tea, the whole time ignoring the frantic voice in my head wondering where she was. "They need to steep," I said, setting the mugs on the table. Anxiously I headed for the stairs. "I'll go up and see what's keeping her."

"But here she comes now."

He was right, for when I glanced up the stairwell, there was Annabelle coming down. She had a dazed look in her eyes, had dressed in jeans and a red blouse, her long hair dancing about her waistline. She moved slowly, as if in a dream.

"There you are," I said. "Didn't you hear me calling?"

She reached the bottom step and took my hand. Her skin was cold, clammy, icy to the touch. She ignored my question, diverting the topic. "Police were here."

My heart stopped.

Dr. Li called from behind me. "Police?"

Annabelle glanced over my shoulder whispering, "Is that him? Is it safe to talk?"

I nodded. "He's safe. Come on, I'll introduce you. But first let me know how you are."

She met my eyes for the first time. "I'm fine, just had another scare. But we might as well talk about it in front of the doctor."

We crossed to the dining table and sat down. "I made you tea," I said.

She thanked me. Dr. Li was watching us, sipping from his mug with a hint of humor in his expression. It was hard to feel stressed or nervous in his presence, and right away I noted this effect on Annabelle. She became less rigid, more relaxed, even regained some of the color in her face.

I cleared my throat and introduced them. They shook hands, smiled. The doctor said, "What's your relationship to the patient?"

"I'm an old friend," she said.

"Ah, like Roger."

"Even older. From childhood."

"Why were the police here, Annabelle?" I asked, not caring if it came off as rude. I was tired of squirming in my own distress.

She looked at me with tired eyes. "They wanted to question him about Celeste's disappearance."

"Did you let them? What happened?" I could hear the anxiety in my voice, but I wanted answers.

"Like this, Roger," the doctor told me, repeating the thrusting motion with his palms, and I performed the movement if only to get him off my back, though I did feel more relaxed after doing it.

"Now, you may speak," he said, bowing toward Annabelle.

She thanked him nervously, then said, "I didn't want to let them in but they were pushy, and plus I was alone and freaking out. When I told them James was too sick to answer questions, they said they'd have to determine that themselves. Otherwise, they'd get a warrant."

I scoffed. "No way could they get a warrant. Based on what?"

"They seemed pretty convinced. They said not allowing them to see James was suspicious."

"Bullshit."

"Annabelle, you did the right thing," Dr. Li said. "When up against people who are using full will, better to follow path of non-resistance—called *wu wei*. That way you're in harmony with nature."

She smiled. I could tell she appreciated the compliment.

But I was growing impatient. "So what happened?"

"I let them in, assuring them James didn't know anything. We went upstairs, into the room, my heart racing. Boy, was it racing. I was sure we'd go in and there would be Celeste and that other girl standing there, alive but dead." She stopped herself, glancing at Dr. Li, curious to see how he reacted, but the doctor only nodded.

"Evil spirits," I offered.

He nodded again.

"Well, were they there?" I asked.

Annabelle shook her head. "Luckily, no. We walked in and James was lying on his side, turned toward the wall. He had the sheet pulled around his shoulders. We tried to wake him, but he was either asleep or faking sleep. After a while he came around. He seemed weak, and I realized he hadn't eaten anything today. The officers tried asking questions, but James said very little. He only nodded and shook his head and grunted. They got a small amount of information this way, from the questions James could answer with a simple yes or no. I think he satisfied them as to how much he knows about Celeste's disappearance—which is nothing. They went away happy."

I took a long, deep breath. "That's a relief. Do you think they'll be back?"

"I don't know, but they gave me their card and said to call if we heard anything. After they left I made James some soup and brought it up to him. I also helped him into the shower, then back into bed."

"How'd that go?"

She paled. "Not too bad… he's different, quieter. He stared at me the whole time with this dazed look in his eyes. Once I saw a flash of something—anger, I think—but that didn't last. But he even started shaking. I thought he was cold so I put him in bed, but he kept on shivering. What do you think about that?"

I considered a moment. "Morphine withdrawals? Seems rather soon."

"He's on morphine?" Dr. Li asked.

"For a few weeks," I said. "But today we… *stopped* the hospital-assigned nurse from giving him another injection. I'm pretty sure James didn't want the stuff, that he was only taking it because he was getting hooked on it—because he *wanted* to die. He'd run out of hope. But yesterday he screamed at the top of his lungs that he wanted to live. I'm of the opinion that morphine and someone who's dying but wants to live have nothing to offer each other. Just my opinion."

"My opinion, too," the doctor said. "How about this nurse? Will she be coming back?"

"We sent her away," I said.

Annabelle added, "We didn't send her. I sort of hit her over the head with a baking pin until she evaporated into thin air."

I cringed as she said this, terrified of Dr. Li's response, but he kept on nodding, smiling.

"We think the nurse was an evil spirit," I said. "She attacked me, and there was something sinister about the morphine regimen she had James on."

"After I struck her, she vanished like smoke," Annabelle said.

Dr. Li sipped his tea, then did a strange thing: sniffed the air. He said, "Yes, I think she was another evil one. The place is infested with them. Your friend is in bad shape."

His words put me so much at ease that I almost wanted to hug him. He was validating what we were telling him, rather than calling us crazy. *He believes us,* I thought. *That means he can probably help us—help James.*

"Pardon me for saying," said Annabelle, "but you don't seem like a doctor. You seem like a priest or a medicine man."

"I'm all of the above," he replied.

"I used to work in a doctor's office, and the people there didn't have many nice things to say about Chinese Medicine."

"Few Westerners do. Some endorse it but most Western doctors have indifferent, negative attitudes. The philosophy behind Chinese medicine is right brain, but Western medicine is left brain. Chinese medicine deals with flows of energy. In the West, they don't believe in energy. All is material, physical. That is why they ridicule us."

"Your card says Esoteric Acupuncture," I said. "What's that?"

"It is acupuncture that has a very specific spiritual foundation. It incorporates the I Ching, the Indian chakra system, ancient Taoist magic, even the Tibetan Book of the Dead. Most comes from my personal experiences. When I was a young man in China I studied under elder grandmaster Chiang Zu. He taught me with vigorous practice much of what I know. The rest I learned through hardship."

I nodded. "Fascinating. You know, I used to have an interest in magic."

"Oh?"

"He used to cast spells for people in college," Annabelle said, smiling. "Spells that helped these people deal with their problems, like completing schoolwork, handling bullies, and getting a date."

I blushed with inferiority. "I studied occult metaphysics and witchcraft," I clarified. "I was quite good, but I've forgotten most of it now."

Dr. Li tapped the side of his head. "It is still in there. Knowledge of the infinite never goes away. And that very good. You may be able to help get us through this. How long ago, you say, in college?"

"That's right, like twenty years ago. It was during the time that James and I attracted the Time Eater."

His bushy eyebrows lifted. "You say, Time Eater?"

"That's our name for the evil spirit because it has a strange effect on time. In a way, its main objective is to devour the past. I think we have quite a story to tell you."

"I'm ready to listen," the doctor said.

Sighing, Annabelle rose from the table. "I think this is going to require more tea."

Chapter Fourteen

We spoke long into the night. Mostly I spoke, though Annabelle contributed when she could. We told the doctor everything down to the finite details, and we didn't hold back. We drank lots of tea while Dr. Li sat calmly, attentively.

When we were done, I glanced at the clock on the wall. "Christ, it's almost ten."

"Do you need to get back to the city, Doctor?" Annabelle asked. "You're welcome to stay in the guest bedroom. Roger can sleep in my room with me."

"He brought his things with him," I said, pointing to the overnight bag.

Dr. Li bowed. "Thank you, I will do that. But first, may I see James?"

"All right," she said. "We should probably head upstairs now, anyway. It's getting late."

She switched off the lights and I helped carry the doctor's bags into the guest bedroom. I removed some clothes from the closet and my suitcase and brought them into Annabelle's room so he would feel like he had the space to himself. We took turns using the bathroom and gathered outside James's door.

"Ready?" she said. We nodded, and she opened the door.

I almost felt the darkness spring out into the hall. It wasn't actually visible, but I felt it *inside my head*, in my thoughts, in my imagination. The others experienced the darkness in a similar way, taking big backward steps as it flowed through the doorway.

"This very bad," Dr. Li said, frowning. He pointed. "In there, is very bad."

"You don't know the half," I said. "You sure you wouldn't rather wait until morning?"

"It's usually less intense during the day," Annabelle added.

But Dr. Li was resolute. He passed between us, taking the lead, and plunged into the room. We followed after.

As usual, everything was black and vast and filled with twinkling stars. In the distance, a series of large, colorful planets rolled aimlessly. In the center, suspended in midair, was the bed; atop that, on his back and staring into space, was James.

He looked severely haggard and shrunken, his beard scraggly, his eyes hollow, his hair flattened and stiff with grease. His bony body poked out of the sheet, the angles protruding here and there like some kind of misshapen skeleton. He heard us enter, turned in our direction, and displayed his yellow teeth.

Dr. Li continued undaunted, approaching James's bed with the stolid presence of an oak tree. We followed behind uneasily. The room felt different, a change in energy, a flux, an incongruity, as though Dr. Li was a monkey wrench in the Time Eater's gears.

At last we all stood before the bed, the doctor in front, gazing down at James like he was a specimen. James looked back with a savage grin. I was convinced the Time Eater had taken control of him completely.

"Who is this, Roger?" he asked. His voice had a harshness to it.

"I am Dr. Li," the doctor said, bowing. "I have waited a long time for this. I've dreamed about you."

James lifted his head. "About me? Have you now, Doc? Not me. Surely…"

"It was you. Since my youth I've had visions of a black emptiness behind the world. For a long time I didn't understand the visions and I'd wake from my sleep, terrified and confused. But I began to see things differently, and once I knew you were there, lurking behind the veil of reality, I knew you were coming for me."

I realized he was addressing the Time Eater itself, not James. This turn of events, with Dr. Li confessing that he was connected to all this, had left me speechless. Why hadn't he mentioned this earlier?

"So there it is…" James said, shrugging in a *What are you gonna do* type of gesture. He seemed to grow more angular, curving like a hook from feet to skull, the front of his face elongating, protruding with a horse's set of yellow teeth. His eyes drew out that rat-like quality, and a shadow passed over the bed.

"Yes, it is the one from my dreams," Dr. Li said, pointing at James but looking at me.

"You knew about this?" I said.

"I suspected but was not certain. I didn't say anything because if I was wrong than I'd be upsetting you unnecessarily. But this is the being I am karmically attached to. It is fate why we are both here, why all of us are here, why you drew attention to this spirit—what you call a Time Eater—in your youth. Everything is linked."

"Listen to that nonsense," James said sarcastically. "Roger, is this guy for real? He talks how you used to talk back at Ohio State." Then he looked at Annabelle and his ferocious eyes grew soft. "Anna, sweetie, was it your idea to bring this wacko here?"

She shook her head. I could tell she was frightened.

"I'm in so much pain, sweetie, I really am," James continued. "I'm dying. You know that I am. So where is Norma, why haven't I gotten my shot today?"

"Norma won't be coming anymore," I said. "Dr. Li is your new primary physician. He's a master acupuncturist."

James's gaze swung toward me. "So this is your idea. Of course it is, you freaky, hippy, New Age faggot. Why couldn't you have stayed shoved up your ex-wife's vagina where you belong?"

A moment of silence. James snickered. "Well, looks like you're here now, eh Doc? But I regret to inform you that all your spiritual efforts are in vain. This one is mine. Everything, all of his life and his past lives, every second he has ever spent incarnated on Earth, is mine. I don't care what kind of portents you've received about me. Try what you like; it will do no good. We of the darkness have claimed him."

The shadow over the bed expanded, stretching in all directions. The pointy tips wrapped like talons around the bedposts and the frame, lifting it higher into the air. The three of us lurched back to get out of the way, as James rose above our heads, laughing. "How can you possibly stick needles in me, Doc, when I'm way up here?"

The doctor turned to us. "That is enough."

I nodded and led us away from the revolving bed, away from the glittering stars looking like eyes, away from the massive presence of those distant planets, and opened the door for us to escape into the hall. As I closed it, the whooshing sound of the bed and the darkness of the room vanished.

I looked at Dr. Li. "What was all that about dreaming? You never mentioned that."

He bowed. "As I said, I have had dreams concerning the formation of reality, and I have had dreams about your friend."

"That was not James," Annabelle said. "That was that thing, the Time Eater."

"She's right. The thing's like a light switch: sometimes it's on, sometimes it's off. But when it's off, Doctor, I'm telling you the real James is scared, terrified, and wants to live."

He considered my words, frowning in the darkness. Finally he said, "I hope you are right, because in order for any of this to work, James's will must be in the right place. Otherwise, he is lost. In my dreams, sometimes everything is swallowed by that horrible encroaching blackness that lurks behind reality... but sometimes it is not."

He bowed again, then padded off to his bedroom and shut the door. I experienced a heavy oppressiveness about my shoulders, an immense burden that was dragging me down. I slouched.

Annabelle picked up on it. Whispering, *"You poor baby,"* she took my hand and led me to her bedroom. I felt like I could sleep a thousand years.

* * *

I dreamed that the doctor and I were running through grass fields. Though he was much older his speed was uncanny, and I struggled to keep up. We hurried across the vast open spaces with strange saggy mountains on either side. Trees, squat and crooked—bonsai trees—sprouted from the soil in places, their trunks and branches smooth. The sky overhead was a deep metallic gray.

"Where are we going, Doc?" I spat between breaths.

He glanced over his shoulder. *"Into the now, Mr. Borough. And from that now... we go into forever."*

We climbed the side of a hill and there at the top, situated among several of the knobby trees, was James's bed with him lying in it. Annabelle kneeled by his head, her skirt spread about her knees in the grass.

Opposite the bed, Celeste and Jenny stood solemnly, draped in robes like druid priestesses. Their faces, young and comely, peered out of the dark spaces beneath their cowls.

Dr. Li came to a stop beside Annabelle. She glanced up, crying. Patting her shoulder, he said, *"This is not about you, my dear. This is about him."* He pointed to James, who was lying motionless on the mattress. The clouds in the sky began to swirl.

"He needs your help to get through this. He needs all of our help." He scanned the lot of us. *"In whatever way our spirits are linked—however we have helped each other during past incarnations—we must call upon that bond now. We must make it the strongest. We six beings have been called together for a reason—to fight that thing out there—"*

He aimed a finger at the sky, and the moment he did the swirling clouds parted. Behind, in the vast patch of blue, a jittering round blob of darkness passed across. Its transparent border quivered, resembling the membrane of a giant cell. Housed within was pure and infinite darkness, spotted with tiny lights and glimmering spheres.

Time Eater, I thought to myself.

Dr. Li said, *"That being is after this particular man's spirit. It wants to devour him, because that's what it does. It is mindless. Only a pure spiritual bond, uniting the six of us, can prevent the being from succeeding. Who is with me?"*

Hands were raised, but while the doctor solemnly acknowledged each, James began to age rapidly in the bed. His body shriveled, growing smaller and smaller, and his skin turned the color of petrified wood. The hair on the top of his head grayed dramatically, and he soon looked like a statue.

I awoke in the brilliant darkness, sweating. For a second I thought I'd been plunged into the Time Eater, that I was being digested in its bottomless well. I sat upright, groping at the space in front of me, and all I kept thinking was, *nothing — nothing — there's nothing!*

A small fire illuminated the darkness: the lamp on Annabelle's side of the bed. Her room was suddenly described to me: her picture frames, clothes, and furniture. A grip fastened on my left shoulder, and I turned sharply.

"It's me!" Annabelle said, flinching. She'd thought I was going to hit her. Maybe I was, but for some strange reason this alone dispelled a great deal of my anxiety. I relaxed, took a breath. In the moments that followed, the fear became a deep-rooted sadness. I felt like crying.

She was there to console me in her matronly way. I was spellbound by her beauty. She was topless. Her skin was soft, pliable, and a sheet of pristine black hair hung over her shoulders. I looked to her face and saw an angel.

"It was only a dream," she said, fingers stroking my cheeks. "You're awake, we're safe now."

"Are we?" My fear was rising again. "Are we safe? What about that?" I nodded in the direction of James's room.

She shook her head, still smiling. "It's relative, of course. And besides, Dr. Li is here now and he's bound to make something happen."

I nodded distractedly, remembering my dream. Finally I was able to let go, and I turned to Annabelle, giving her my attention.

I kissed her, afraid she'd withdraw, but instead she reciprocated. In a moment my hands were cupping her breasts, our tongues playing tug-o-war, her fingers dragging down the back of my neck.

She pulled away. "I haven't slept with a man for a long time. And you know that if we sleep together, everything will change. I have to be prepared for that."

"I'm positive that it's been *longer* for me," I said. "Things'll change, but they might change for the better." I almost laughed, hearing myself. Who was talking? Certainly not Roger Borough, divorcee, fourteen-years-long single man who hated women and had given up on them, who'd grown bitter and sullen—no, certainly not him.

We slid underneath the covers, my heart beating so fast I thought I might choke on it. The feeling of her naked flesh pressed against mine was almost too much. I grew aroused, the throbbing down there aching to be inside her.

I can't believe it. After all these years... The smile on my face was so wide I felt embarrassed and switched off the lamp. But Annabelle hadn't noticed. She was caught in the passion of the moment. Opening her legs, her knees poked out of the covers, black hair staining the white pillows. She grabbed my hips and guided me into position, pausing to whisper in my ear, *"I want you, Roger. It's been so long..."*

We made love quickly, rashly, fitfully, but with a growing urgency. We stopped and breathed, while I lay collapsed on her chest. We didn't speak. As the night wore on, soon, just as I thought we were both falling asleep, we made love again. Softly, slowly, gracefully. This went on for some time.

Chapter Fifteen

Sun poured through the window, gilding the wood furniture, illuminating motes of dust. In the back of my head, a voice reminded me, *You had sex with a woman last night,* and I grinned instantly.

I selected new clothes, hit the shower, glancing at the wall clock on my way into the hall. It was eight o'clock.

I smelled breakfast as I came down the stairs, found Annabelle and Dr. Li sitting at the kitchen table. She'd whipped up eggs and toast and hash browns, bacon, and waffles. Even fresh-squeezed orange juice.

What's gotten into her?

When she looked up and met my eyes, I knew she was feeling as happy and excited as I was. We shared a brief moment from which the rest of the world was excluded. Annabelle and I had a secret knowledge about why we were in such high spirits. *I could get used to this,* I thought.

"Good morning, Roger," she said. "I made you a plate."

I sat down and thanked her. She gave me a kiss on the cheek, then started washing some dishes.

"Morning, Doctor," I said.

"Good morning, Mr. Borough."

"How'd you sleep?"

He hesitated. "Not well."

Annabelle came over to refill his mug with coffee. In that red apron, she looked almost like a waitress in a diner. "He had nightmares," she informed me.

Dr. Li thanked her, then said, "Not exactly nightmares, but *visions.* Meetings on the spiritual plane. There is here, the material plane—" he thumped the table with two knuckles "—and there are the higher spiritual worlds." He pointed toward the ceiling.

"The spirit realm," I said.

"While my physical body lay here, asleep in the bed in the guest room, my astral body was out there, with the spirits, sort of floating around. That's what the soul does during sleep: it becomes disconnected from the physical foundation and crosses to the sea of infinity. That's why we dream—it's what our bodiless minds glimpse while we're over there. Sort of like LSD."

"Turn on, tune in, drop out," Annabelle said, joining us at the table. She had her own coffee and was sipping it.

"That's Timothy Leary," I said between mouthfuls. "By the way, the breakfast is amazing."

She smiled at me. "I am glad you're enjoying it." Then she turned to the doctor. "Didn't mean to interrupt. You were saying?"

"I was talking about the two worlds, the material and the spiritual. Last night I met with you all in the spirit realm. James was there. Also the missing woman, Celeste, and your ex-wife, Jenny. The Time Eater was present."

I dropped my fork, which clanged against the plate. "Holy shit, I had the same dream."

Dr. Li nodded. "Yes, I thought so. Your presence was strongest of the group. What I realized from this vision is that James's spirit, not his physical body, is sick. To heal him, we must battle for his soul."

We were quiet a while, absorbing this information. After breakfast, we went out to the backyard to have tea. The house had a large wood deck extending into the grass. We sat around a large square glass table, beneath some shade from a tree.

"Where do we start?" I said.

Dr. Li reached into the pocket of his shirt, withdrawing something small that I mistook for a cigarette. He lit it with a lighter, setting it in the ashtray on the table, and I realized it was incense. A thin line of smoke twisted upward, smelling strong and unpleasant.

He looked at me. "We begin with you, actually."

"What do you mean?"

"Before we can hope to get at the Time Eater, we must incapacitate the other suffering spirit."

I suddenly understood what he was talking about and my heartbeat fluttered. "You mean Jenny, don't you?'

He nodded. "James took care of the other spirit, his ex-wife Celeste. Now it is up to you to handle this one. You must face her, Roger."

Annabelle touched my hand. I nearly jumped out of my skin. The very idea of seeing Jenny again terrified me. Annabelle touched my hand again; this time I let her. "I'm here," she said.

"I'm not sure I can do it," I said. My voice had gone shaky. "I don't know what power that woman has over me, but it rules me with an iron fist. It controlled my life while we were married, and even afterward it controlled me. I was resigned not to get involved with another woman because of it."

I glanced at Annabelle to determine her expression, but her eyes were unreadable. *She thinks I'm still in love with Jenny,* I thought.

Dr. Li took hold of the incense, waved it before my face. I wrinkled my nose at the odious smell. "Christ, what is that stuff?"

He smiled. "Very special moxa stick. Can't be found anywhere but in China. And only certain people know how to make it."

"Let me guess. You're one of those people."

His smile widened. "Moxa's most common use is for the smoothing of blood and qi flow. But with this, I see into the heart of one's blood and qi. Past it even. Into one's soul."

Using his hand, he waved the smoke in my direction. It began to curl around my arms like a snake's tail, around my neck and head. I felt my eyes water.

Annabelle gasped, took her hand off mine, and put it over her mouth.

"What is it?" I said, panicking.

She shook her head. Then pointed. "I can see her face. It's right there with your face—I can see you both, like hers is superimposed on top of yours."

"What?"

I whipped my head toward Dr. Li. Very calmly and casually, he flicked his wrist until the moxa extinguished and placed it back in the ashtray.

"This woman Jenny has attached herself to your soul," he said. "The moxa reveals it as such. This is why her will has been able to control you even after her physical presence has gone. Her essence grafted onto you and a projection of her is inside your mind. This is not healthy."

Jenny's voice boomed in my head like a loudspeaker. *Don't listen to him! No baby, don't listen. Listen to Mommy. You need me, you always have. You never grew up and you never really became a man because you're over-attached to—really in love with—your deceased mother. It's simple psychology, love, Oedipus 101. I've done my best to make you aware of it.*

I hated that. I hated everything she used to tell me, that she used to whisper in my ear as we lay in bed at night after sex. All of her insidious, psychological probing, which enabled her to have total knowledge of my inner world. *Gnosis,* she'd called it in a sick, condescending tone. A great scheme to take control of me.

I jumped to my feet, picking up my chair and heaving off the deck into the grass. It tumbled twice before coming to a halt, scattering the birds from the tree.

"*No!*" I screamed, slapping my face with my hands. I could feel Jenny all through me—her smell, her taste, her touch—like we were the same person. I wanted her out.

Annabelle dashed across the wood planks. "Stop it, Roger, Jesus!"

"*No!*" I kept clawing at my cheeks, even after Annabelle had her arms around me. "*I can't take it anymore!*"

But Annabelle refused to give up. She was surprisingly strong, too, managing to pull my arms down and pin them to her chest. I had my eyes closed, shaking my head, but she got right into my face. "Remember last night, Roger. You're with me now. Goddamn it, *remember!*"

She slapped me, hard, and like that Jenny's presence disappeared. I felt it leak away like water through a sieve. I clasped my arms around Annabelle's waist, starting to cry. Gently, she stroked my head and led me back to the table.

Time passed. When I felt calm, I said, "What must I do?"

Dr. Li was sitting with lidded eyes, looking off into the trees. Sunlight through the branches painted the grass. He seemed to be listening to something only he could hear.

"We must send you into the spirit realm. Once you are there, you'll have to attract your ex-wife's attention. Then…" he trailed off.

"Then *what*?"

He glanced at me, still smiling, and made a chopping motion with his hand. "You cut off her head."

I burst out laughing. "You can't be serious. How am I supposed to cut off the head of a spirit?"

"Roger, give it a chance," Annabelle said.

"It's not real head," Dr. Li explained. "It's just a metaphysical head. Trust me, you'll know what to do. But first I must prepare an herbal tonic that will sedate you and allow you to cross over. I'll need to use your kitchen."

"Of course." Annabelle got up and accompanied the doctor inside. Before disappearing completely, she turned to me and said, "You gonna be all right?"

I nodded, and she slipped into the house.

Am *I going to be all right?* An abyss had opened under my feet. I felt like those tightrope walkers, the ones who strung ropes between two skyscrapers. No safety net waited to catch me if I fell into the abyss. There was only one way to go—down.

I was in a strange place mentally. I was happy I'd come here to be with James because it had enabled Annabelle and me to meet; it also allowed me to rediscover huge gaps in my past, things I'd forgotten or intentionally blocked out. I was excited and hopeful about helping James overcome his illness.

But I felt lost, like I was no longer myself. The last fourteen years of my life had been spent in biter solitude; work and TV made up my social life. Sometimes I'd befriend one of my students, but even that always remained a professional relationship. I'd grown very comfortable being alone, and I'd conditioned myself to not focus on Jenny.

Now everything was in motion, spinning around, faster and faster. I'd become conscious of the magnitude of the situation and there was no going back.

A halting shape in the grass caught my attention and I turned… and just about swallowed my tongue. James was standing there in his grubby pajamas—more like a formless image than a person. Mist swirled around him. He was a rat-like apparition, limbs and face curving downward into a beak, grinning at me.

"What the hell do you want?" I said under my breath. He continued to show his teeth, the mist circling around him.

"I know it's my fault, is that what you want?"

He said nothing.

"I got us into this mess at Ohio State, I drew the attention of that *thing*, that eater of time that's got you by the balls, but now I've come back to help you out, man. I even went and found some esoteric Chinese healer. What more do you want from me?"

His grin faltered, his body flickered. For a moment, he resembled something out of a silent film. Lifting his hand, he pointed toward the trees at the rear of the backyard.

I followed his finger, seeing nothing out of the ordinary. I shook my head. But that's when a massive blotch of color began spreading across the trunks, an expanding purple orb that engulfed the greenness and blocked everything out.

Glued to the chair, I watched as a strange landscape took shape within the opening. I saw purple mountain-like forms in the distance; a purple sun couched in a purple sky; the terrain dotted here and there with black boulders and what might have been black shrubs.

Intuitively, I knew I was looking into the spirit world. It was like the surface of a dead planet, a wasteland of purple and black, an abstract rendering painted by an artist who'd gone insane. Out of this insanity stepped Jenny, my ex-wife.

She was tall and emaciated. Her blonde hair appeared ghostly in its waviness. She was naked except for a red scarf (*I remember that scarf, it's* the one her mother gave to her when her father was killed in the war) wrapped around her neck, dangling between her breasts. She moved like a lithe ballerina across the grass.

We made eye contact, those crystal blues of hers, so discerning and inquisitive. I could all but hear her whispering, *Tell me. Tell me all that you remember from childhood. Married couples share things with each other, Roger. I can help you…*

"No, no, no," I began to mutter without realizing it. She filled me with such impotent rage and hatred—mixed, paradoxically, with devout loyalty and longing—that I suddenly just wished she would go away.

At that instant James's swirling form lunged at her. He held out his fingers, which melted into hard iron, a rusted blade of minerals and flesh. He sort of danced in a circle, bringing the blade around Jenny's neck in a graceful arc. She had a single moment to mouth the words *Help Me* before James took her head clean off. It dropped to the grass with a thud, rolled, her body crumpling after. Blood gushed in waves and stained the grass a dark, sensuous red.

I got up from the chair and went inside.

Chapter Sixteen

Annabelle and Dr. Li were busy in the kitchen. The doctor had opened his medical bag on the dining table, had spread out its contents. I took a moment to look it all over: a collection of jars labeled with Chinese characters, each containing strange-looking herbs; an array of small glass cups; more moxa sticks; books and what resembled papyrus scrolls; and a huge Zip-lock bag full of tiny needles, each individually packaged and sanitized.

"Did anyone bring James his breakfast?" I asked.

They looked at me. Annabelle pointed to the counter, where a plate of food sat cooling. "I was afraid to go in there."

"I'll take care of it." I snatched up the plate and headed upstairs. I entered James's bedroom, crossing the carpet floor, and began yanking the drapes open, freeing the sunlight.

James, a musky packrat lying in bed, groaned and turned onto his side when I opened the window. "Get out," he mumbled. "Just let me die. I've had enough."

I sat in the chair by the bed. "Eat this."

He raised a hand over his shoulder and flipped me the bird.

"Goddam it, James, eat it." I grabbed the sheet and pulled it off him, exposing his long, bony body darkened by the first hints of bedsores.

He laboriously got in a seated position, retrieving the sheet to wrap it around his waist. I couldn't believe how thin he was. I searched his face for signs of the Time Eater, but it seemed like I was actually looking at James. I sighed with relief. Maybe I could actually talk to him.

I held out the plate and he took it, began shoveling the eggs and potatoes into his mouth. Bits of yellow and brown got lodged in his beard. I didn't say a word until he was finished, for I knew he could only eat when the Time Eater wasn't controlling him.

He gave the plate back to me, scraped clean. I set it on the floor. His expression softened. "Thanks," he said. "I needed that. Help an old pal to the bathroom?"

I smiled, glad that he'd asked. "Sure."

His body felt like a sack of brittle sticks as he threw his arm around my neck. I supported him until we had reached the bathroom. A horrible odor of urine emanated from him.

"I can take it from here," he said, detaching from me and sort of limping though the door and closing it behind him. "Gonna be a minute," he called. "You might as well get comfy. I need a shower."

"You got it, pal." I had a seat by the window. I slid open the glass, letting fresh air in. Warm, summer air, full of moist humidity. Brooklyn was out there, sounds and the wavering sea of rooftops, the buildings and the trees and the grass plots and chain-link fences.

I drifted while I watched the world going by. James's voice snapped me out of it. "Hey, you fall asleep? I said I'm ready."

"Yeah, sorry, coming."

I opened the bathroom door where he was bracing himself against the frame. A cloud of steam wafted out. I glanced past him and saw clothes and dirt had begun to build up on the tile floor. The sink was quite dirty, and I wondered if it would be a good idea to run a wet rag over the place.

He curled his arm across my shoulders again, and we headed to the bed. He got himself situated, and then I pulled the sheets over him. "You don't need a blanket?" I asked.

"Fuck no. It's damn hot in here."

"Well I can leave the windows open."

He didn't answer, but eventually said, "Just make sure you shut the drapes. I don't like all this sun. I can't stand it."

"You don't think it's nice?" I chuckled at his general bad attitude.

"What's the point? Where I'm going, there isn't going to be any sun. Might as well get used to it."

"That's bullshit." But I did as he asked, closing the drapes and consigning the room to darkness. It felt like a tomb.

"What about my shot?" he said.

Of course. He wants his morphine.

"Might be some later," I lied. "For now why don't you take it easy."

"It's because of that new doctor. The Chinese fellow. I had a dream about him last night."

"His name is Dr. Li and he's very good. He's going to help us get through this."

James grunted as if to say *I'll believe it when it happens.* He rolled over and proclaimed with finality, "Now I sleep."

"Fine. I'll leave you alone." I picked up the empty plate and went for the door, but before I could escape into the hall I felt compelled to tell him, "You know, today it's my turn to face the demons."

"Yeah, I know," he said, almost irritably. "You're gonna get rid of that bitch who made a lapdog out of you. All I can say is good riddance."

"That's about all I have to say, too." I slipped through the door, pulling it closed behind me.

Annabelle and Dr. Li appeared to be finishing up whatever they'd been doing.

"What took so long?" she asked.

I set the plate on the counter. "I helped him into the bathroom and he took a shower. We also talked a bit. He seemed his old self again… sort of."

She smiled. "That's great, Roger. Really great." Then Dr. Li cleared his throat, prompting her to say, "Oh, we're ready for you. The tonic's finished."

I bent over the table where the doctor was sitting and sniffed the mug of steaming liquid that was before him. I wrinkled my nose. It smelled like a sour foot. "What in the name of God is it?"

"It's special, just for you," he answered. Then he rattled off a list of herbs with Asian-sounding names, few of which I recognized. "In order for it to work," he said, "you must drink it in a special place, a place chosen by you alone. Do you have a place in mind?"

I nodded, "I do," then snatched the mug and headed into the backyard. They followed me out and stood watching me with inquiring eyes. "After you two went inside," I explained, "I had a vision out here. I saw an opening to the spirit world and I saw Jenny walk out of it."

Dr. Li's bushy eyebrows lifted. "You did? Where?"

I pointed to the line of trees near the back of the yard. He nodded and began to walk in that direction, signaling us to join him. When we reached the trees, I pointed to the grass and said, "Right here."

I sat down with Annabelle and the doctor standing over me and commenced drinking the tonic. But after the first sip I nearly dumped the whole thing out. "It tastes like rancid meat," I said.

"That 'cause it's very good," the doctor replied, smiling.

Annabelle kneeled beside me, placing a hand on my shoulder. "Go on," she said, "You can do it."

I filled myself with resolution and gulped it down, gagging after I had finished. "Stuff'll kill someone," I muttered. Immediately I got lightheaded and toppled back in the grass, dropping the mug. Looking up at the sky through the branches, the world began to spin.

The last thing I saw before slipping into darkness was Dr. Li's wise old face peering down at me.

* * *

"Is that it? Has he flipped to the other side?"
"Yes, he is gone. Now come. We have much to do…"

* * *

I was surrounded by the warmth of a woman. She had her arms around me, clutching me to her chest. The slow steady draw of her soft flesh called to me, and I wanted nothing more than to be sheltered inside it. I began clawing, pulling at it and stretching it tight. I yanked it down over my head, over my naked body, and like a piece of chewed bubble gum it stuck to my skin, encapsulating me. I opened my mouth and took a breath.

Then I opened my eyes.

What is this?

Where am I?

I had returned to the seething purple landscape dotted with black boulders and shrubs.

Returned?

Yes, I had been here before. Long before I was born.

The sky—no, not sky, more sea-like—over my head pulsated and heaved. It looked like dark water thrashing in a bowl. I was on my back but now got up to my feet. The pain in my limbs was unbearable. When I evaluated myself, I almost went into shock. I had become something different. I was no longer Roger Borough but an alien, with pale skin stretched over thin bones, hands large as dinner plates, feet like a giant's, and tall as a tree.

I heard a voice, soft and lilting—a female voice—calling out to me, and it reminded me why I was here: James, Dr. Li, Annabelle, the spirit world.

Jenny.

* * *

There she went, disappearing over the top of a large purple hill. Her voice, soft like a child's, flickered back to me.

"You'll never catch me."

Courage flooded my twisted alien veins, and a warrior's blood pumped in my heart. *We'll see about that,* I thought, starting after her.

The limbs and joints in my new body moved with startling ease, despite their size. More loping than walking. My arms hung down apelike, knuckles dragging on the ground. By accident I realized I had the ability to *sharpen* my arms, elongate them, hands tapering to two points. Like swords.

I remembered Dr. Li saying, *It's not her literal head you must cut off, but her metaphysical one.*

I spent a few moments altering them back and forth—blades, arms, blades, arms—then grinned as I proceeded up the hill.

After reaching the top, I came face-to-face with a vision of such astounding power. I stood awe-struck, surveying the view I had attained from this height. The stony purple landscape stretched in all directions, merging with the distant horizon and transforming into sky. Piles of black boulders lay scattered everywhere, often ringing the mouths of dark, gaping pits. Shrubs and trees, also black, possessed a counterfeit quality, like cardboard cutouts.

"Over here," she called.

My eyes left the vast tumbling cloud-beast shapes in the sky to find Jenny sitting under a paper-thin tree. To her left, a large black stone was propped up ceremoniously in the dirt, ringed by smaller stones.

Jenny looked like I did—that is, she was tall, thin, bony and white, naked with large hands and feet. Her face was wide, eyes deep-set, mouth full and inviting, and her blonde hair swam off the back of her head as though pulled by the wind, although the air was still.

For some reason, because we had both adopted this alien form, I was not afraid of her. We now appeared evenly matched, at least in my eyes. That hard beautiful shell she'd worn on the outside of her skin, which for years had both repulsed and attracted me, was gone; without it she seemed kinder, gentler.

"Come and sit down," she said.

Before I had time to think, I was already moving. *That's how it is with us,* I thought. *She says jump, I say how high.*

But I sat down, tucking my lengthy appendages beneath me, as she displayed her strange etheric countenance, with a world of cosmic blacks and blues around us. For an absurd moment I felt like I was on the cover of a cheesy science fiction novel, and I laughed.

Tilting her head, she said, "What's so funny?"

I gestured. "All *this*. How ridiculous it is." But then I stopped, having a sudden clarity, and continued—"It's like I know so much now. So many new ideas are popping up in my head."

"Why don't you tell me about them?"

"I can remember my past lives. Jesus, they are countless." I chuckled. "In one I was an Arabian *sheikh* and I think James was my son. In another I lived in a small village in Africa… and you were there." I paused. "Holy shit, you were my mother."

"Human incarnations are linked. The cycle of death and rebirth is what turns the Karmic wheel. The past is important, but it can also become a prison. We can easily get stuck in it, and then we're frozen in time. That's what the Time Eater is for."

"It eats away the past," I said. "It forces us to live in the present."

She nodded.

"You make it sound like a good thing," I said.

"It's an essential thing."

"But it eats away the present, too, I know it does. I've witnessed it."

"The Time Eater is mindless. It does what it does without thinking. As each second passes, the present becomes the past. Think of the Time Eater as an algae-eating fish in a giant aquarium. As long as there's food, it'll keep eating."

I looked down at my giant clawed hands. "It's going to eat James."

She was quiet and I could feel the tension in her. Some force was building. I suspected she wanted to tell me something but was afraid to. At last she said, "That is one possibility. The two of you are so funny, you know that? My God, don't you even remember?"

I looked at her. "Remember what?"

She sighed. "I can't tell you, Roger. You'll have to find out for yourself." She held her arms out to me, long sinewy stalks connected to a tight pale chest with small breasts. I knew she desired to embrace me. I could feel the draw, the pull, the tractor beam of intensity that wanted to fuse us together. I tried to fight the urge, but my will was weak and like a child I crawled into her lap and curled up against her. We sat for a long time. I felt comfortable in her arms, so warm, so safe.

"Do you remember our trip to China?" I said.

She made a noise of surprise in her throat. "I haven't thought of that in ages."

"I thought about it recently. If I had to pick the happiest moment of our marriage, it would be there, in the City of Ghosts. I felt close to you then."

She held me tighter and stroked my head. "You can feel close to me now, here. You never have to leave, Roger. You can stay with me forever, frozen in time. We'll be happy, just like old times. You know I love you."

I nearly burst into tears. Reaching up, I curled one of my arms around her neck to give her a hug. "I love you too, Jenny. For so long I wanted to be here, *right here*, with you, never leaving. I wanted us to be together like we were in China. I wanted that moment to last forever."

"It can, darling, it can. If you stay with me—if you stay with Mommy—the world will move along without us and we can dwell in the past, free of time. All you have to do is let it go. Let it *all* go."

"I have wanted this so much…" I muttered. "I have wanted you to come back to me so we could be together. But now…" I morphed my hand into a blade behind her head. "Now everything is different."

She shushed me. "No, sweetheart, no. Nothing is different. We *can* be together. We can make it last forever. Remember, I know what's best."

But at this crucial moment I was able to summon my courage, my warrior, my strength. I remembered Annabelle. I remembered James. I remembered myself.

"I'm sorry," I said, tears in my eyes, "but I refuse to live in the past. I refuse to give in to my own suffering." I very gently brought the blade down across her neck. It sliced through her flesh. Her eyes regarded me for a moment before she opened her mouth to say something. Then the head fell into my lap and I screamed.

Her corpse tipped forward, spewing black, purple blood. I pushed her off me and jumped to my feet, casting away the severed head as though it were a loathsome insect. I looked at her sagging body, now lying in a puddle of blood.

The sky darkened. Stars and planets blinked to life, and right then I knew—God help me, *I knew*—the Time Eater was coming. It was on to me, but it was also too late. I had already done what I had come here to do. I had severed Jenny's hold on my soul. I had stepped out of the past.

As its massive shadow crept across the land, I fell to me knees, face aimed at the sky.

* * *

When I came to, the doctor was leaning over me. His bushy eyes and wrinkled face were all I could see, and he smelled of incense and herbs. When he saw my eyes open, he smiled. "Ah, here he comes."

He pulled back, and when he did the sky and trees and branches and colors all swung into view. Annabelle was kneeling behind him in the grass. Her pretty face was corrupted by worry. The wind had seized her long black hair, was stretching it out behind her… reminding me of Jenny.

She touched my arm, fingers cold. "How do you feel, Roger?"

My heart was thundering. I felt the icy chill of a cold sweat over my body. Remembering the strange alien form I had inhabited in the spirit world, I sat up very quickly to inspect myself. To my relief, I inhabited my old flesh and bones again.

"Oh Christ," I said. "Christ, I did it. I cut off her head. It was... horrible—but it felt great!"

Dr. Li patted my shoulder. "You did good, Mr. Borough. I'm proud of you. Now we can proceed to the next step." He rose cautiously to his feet, careful of his joints. Annabelle helped me and supported me because my legs felt like Jell-O. We made our way across the yard to the house. Judging by the sunlight, it was well past noon.

"What *is* the next step?" Annabelle said.

Dr. Li pointed to the upstairs window—to James's bedroom. Annabelle and I both gasped simultaneously as we looked and saw James's peaked face hovering in the glass. Ghostlike, his complexion pale, his eyes void-black. He watched us.

The doctor said, "Next step is getting inside your friend and seeing where the Time Eater has dug its hooks into him."

We went inside and Annabelle made some hot tea. I still felt very tired, and I spent much of the afternoon on the couch, watching episodes of *Have Gun Will Travel* on the TV while she and the doctor spoke in the kitchen. She was helping him prepare more herbs, I suspected. A little while later, I dozed again.

Chapter Seventeen

The TV blared an annoying commercial for the evening news, and I got up and quickly switched it off. The house was dimly lit with a few lamps and the purplish light of twilight in the windows. I listened, waiting to hear either the doctor or Annabelle, but there was nothing.

Shit, maybe they started without me. I panicked, then thought, *Shit, maybe they started without me and failed and now they're up there being torn to shreds!*

I jumped to my feet and ran into the kitchen. The place was a mess, pots and pans everywhere, jars of herbs, books outspread, and curious glass containers. Dr. Li's medical bag was open with its contents spewing out. They'd been busy, whatever they were doing. I was about to rush upstairs when I happened to glance out the window. The car was not in the driveway.

They went somewhere?

I decided to go upstairs anyway and check. As I ascended the darkening staircase, I shivered. I'd really grown to hate coming up here. Every time I wanted to fool myself, thinking everything was back to normal, I'd come up here and all hell would break loose.

I opened James's bedroom door and peered in. The moment I did, the lights sprang on. The window facing the backyard was open; a stream of purple twilight flowed in, mixing with the artificial light to create a murky ambience.

He was sitting up in the bed, back to the wall, reading a book that at once looked familiar. He pretended not to notice me, but I knew he was only pretending. My attention focused on the large leather bound book with white pages and gold trim, which he read with furious intensity, flipping the pages.

Holy crap, is that…?

He glanced up. His eyes burned me down, voided and dead, his face taking on the characteristics of a rodent.

He's with the Time Eater.

"Oh, it's you," he said. "Guess what I found."

I stepped inside, closing the door behind me. I made a quick scan of the room to be sure Annabelle and the doctor were not here.

"Come close," he said, indicating the chair beside the bed. "Your favorite spot."

I wasn't used to this room appearing so bright, could not recall seeing it with this many lights on. A cold, uninviting glare, the kind of illumination you find in a hospital: sterilized, clinical.

I did as he asked, but even as I sat down my eyes never left the book.

James noticed me looking and smiled. "Has it crossed your mind yet, pal? This thing ringing any bells?" He shook the book at me. "Let me give you a hint, you're gonna have to go back. *Way* back."

Just like that I knew. Like I had plucked it out of the air. I said, "No fucking… it can't be. Is it? Where the hell did you get it?"

My reaction pleased him, and he laughed. "You do remember. This is how it all started, isn't it? Where we first blurred the line between reality and fiction, past and present…" He paused before adding, "Between you and me."

James flipped through the pages, reading again, pretending like I wasn't even there. For an instant, my eyes lighted upon the title, embroidered on the leather cover in gold letters. It was Latin, but I remembered that Randolf, owner of the occult bookstore I haunted in college, had translated it for me. Roughly, it worked out to *Sprit of the Infinite and the Solomonic Key to Christ.*

"Here's an interesting passage," James said, reading aloud in Latin. The foreign words and complex declensions filled the room. He sounded like a monk in a monastery, and a few of the words I recognized, though it had been so long since I studied Latin, and I knew for a fact that James couldn't read it.

He stopped and looked up. "Any of this sound familiar?"

"You know it doesn't. It's not English."

He scoffed. "But you were able to read it that night. Yes, you read it fluently, not once second-guessing yourself. Your voice echoed off the tall campus buildings. I can remember it. Eerie shit, man."

I was starting to get confused. "But I never took classes, never had any proper instruction in Latin."

"But you spoke it. You said the owner of that weird little bookstore taught you."

He turned the book around, offered it to me, temptingly. "Come on, if I can do it, you can do it. Try it. See if you remember."

I reached for the book, but he immediately pulled it away and laughed. "Have to do better than that, pal. Looks like I'm the only one capable of speaking Latin around here."

"The way you speak it is unnatural. It's not really you speaking it. It's that thing."

He made a face as if to say, *And your point is…*, then went back to reading aloud. As his voice stirred the air, I noticed the walls begin to grow thin, transparent, to flicker like images on a movie screen. One by one, they faded out.

James kept reading as the world turned pitch-black. The stars and planets glimmered to life, the cosmic mists flowed in from the distance, and the asteroid belts rolled imperceptibly. I shivered. We were in *its* territory now.

"Stop it, James," I said, growing more afraid. "Stop reading it. You'll draw its attention."

He paused. "That didn't stop you that night." Then continued.

Our world swelled with darkness. Any moment the Time Eater would be here. And then what? What would happen if, when the being started sucking things into itself, we stayed put and didn't move? Would it eventually siphon us away as well?

I need to get my hands on that book. Even if I can't read it, I've got to get it away from him.

A section of reality to our left tumbled down, huge transparent chunks of space and stars toppling over like kids' blocks; they kept falling, down and down, into oblivion.

"Goddamn it, James, stop!" I approached the bed. The moment my knee touched the mattress, he went berserk, yelling and cursing, clutching the book to his chest, showing me his teeth.

"Fuck… the hell away from me!" he screeched. He spit and the fluid struck my face, getting into my eyes. I can't say I was surprised by his behavior; however, the abruptness of it sent me into high alert. Meanwhile, a massive warbling presence was taking shape behind the falling reality blocks, something sensed more than seen, a thing black and vast and mindless.

"Give it, James," I said, groping at him. He'd tucked himself into a fetal position with the book at his chest. When I reached for it, he actually tried to bite me; on impulse I slapped him hard in the face. Drops of saliva pelted the sheets, but he was momentarily stunned.

I jumped on the opportunity and snatched the book from his grip. As it left him, he let out a wail that sent shivers up my spine. I turned immediately and stalked toward the door.

"No!" he called after. "I found it, not you! I thought about it until it appeared in my hands and now you come to take it away from me—not fair!"

I couldn't help glancing in the direction of the tumbling reality blocks on my way out. Big mistake. I was held captive by a vision of the Time Eater. Black and massive, more like the view of a distant horizon than any organic creature; it stretched back as far as I could see. It resembled something I'd once perceived under a microscope in a Petri dish, a single-cell organism, a bacteria, an amoeba. A giant inkblot trembling in a neon purple membrane, with eyes and a set of teeth—maybe? No… all blackness there. Nothing more.

I hurried out into the hall.

Chapter Eighteen

I sat at the kitchen table for the next hour poring over the text. It felt strange to hold this book in my hands again after so many years. A flood of memories came back from those years I had forgotten, my time spent as an occult practitioner. I recalled the people I helped in college, how I solved their problems using magic and intuition.

The memories seemed unreal, as if they'd happened to someone else. At that time, I was so immersed in magic that I never gave it a second thought, but from this angle, it felt surreal.

Who am I really? I kept thinking, and the scariest part was I had no idea.

When the car pulled up in the driveway, I had the book set on the table and was staring at it. For the life of me, I couldn't decipher a single phrase of the text. If I was so able to read Latin once, I couldn't understand why the ability was now lost to me.

Annabelle and Dr. Li came through the door, saw me sitting at the table. They were each carrying a brown shopping bag, which they put on the countertop. Dr. Li noticed the book almost immediately, his eyes going wide.

"You're up," Annabelle said. "Feeling better?"

"A little. Where'd you go?"

"The store to get more ingredients," the doctor said. "There are certain things required for a Chinese medical practitioner to do his work." He hoisted out a six-pack of diet Pepsi. "Like diet soda."

I laughed. "Ancient Chinese secret?"

"Yes." He sat down in the chair across from me and picked up the book. The second his hands touched it, his expression changed and his face went pale. "Where'd this come from?" he said.

I pointed to the ceiling. "James."

"You saw him," Annabelle asked. "How'd he look?"

I shuddered, remembering the way he had snapped at me when I tried to take the book from him. "Not good. But he had that." I indicated the book. "He said he found it. But I haven't set eyes on it in twenty years."

"You've seen it before?" Dr. Li asked.

I nodded. "That's the book I was telling you about, the one James and I used to summon the Time Eater. After going to *Cosmos, Psyche, and Higher Worlds* I thought it was a lost cause, but now James turns up this copy. The strangest part is I think it's the *same* copy we used in college."

Annabelle joined us at the table, carrying the soda, a bowl of ice, and three glasses. "How can you tell?"

"May I?" I retrieved the book from Dr. Li, opened to about the middle where a bunch of the text was underlined in black, and showed it to her. "I remember doing that on the night of the ritual. When I performed the chants, the text would seem to blur together, trip me up. Underlining it kept me on track."

I passed it back to the doctor so he could continue looking. Then Annabelle said, "How do you suppose James got it?"

"I've been thinking about that. Most of that night on the Ohio State campus is a blur. But I do recall the misplacement of the book after the ritual was over. I threw away all of my occult paraphernalia the next day, vowing never to practice magic. But the book... it was gone. I never had a chance to toss it. My guess is that James snuck it home for whatever reason. And he's held on to it ever since."

"That would make sense," she said.

"What do you think, Doctor?" I asked.

He was silent. Finally, he placed it on the table and took a sip from the glass of soda Annabelle had poured for him. "I lived in China until I was about twenty-nine, in a tiny village in the Hunan province. My parents were farmers for a burgeoning company. They saved enough money for me to attend college, and this I did, all the way in Hong Kong. But in my younger days, I studied under the elder grandmaster of the village, Chiang Zu, whom I have already mentioned to you. He was very wise, knew many things. Sometimes he took me into mountains to practice acupuncture on animals."

He paused, pointing at the book. "We found something just like that half-buried in a pile of rotting bamboo."

"Get out of here," I said. "This exact book?"

He inspected it again, as if to be certain, then nodded. "I remember the funny shapes of the words, and this…" He opened the back flap to where a gold engraving had been stitched into the binding. It was a curious symbol, one that surpassed even my knowledge of the occult. It depicted three triangles—one upright, the others placed above and angled down, one to either side, all three points touching.

"What's it mean?" Annabelle asked.

I shrugged. "Beats me. I have the faintest recollection of Randolf telling me something about it, but I don't recall." I looked at Dr. Li. "Do you know?"

"I only know what Master Chiang told me. The day we found it, we had been searching for sick animals to heal. We came upon a vast expanse of fallen bamboo. I knew it had recently been cut down, because the blade marks were still fresh. Resting on top of the pile was that book.

"My master grew very still, very tense. I had never observed him to be so nervous. He crossed the bamboo and lifted the book from its resting place. When he returned, he flipped through the pages and showed me this engraving in the back. He said that Taoist wizards sometimes poked their noses into places they didn't belong—dark places, evil places. He recognized the symbol, but he did not relate to me its origin. He did, however, decipher it.

"He told me that the human organism is composed of three parts: the spirit, soul, and body. The spirit goes through different incarnations, and it is eternal, infinite. The soul is the personality of the present incarnation. The body, well, that is self-explanatory—it's the vehicle. Each triangle in the engraving represents one of the three. If you noticed, three triangles together form another triangle. A forth triangle. This is the fourth whole. Divinity."

I picked up the book and flipped to the back. Sure enough, the engraving depicted four triangles total. I thought that I remembered something about this, but the memory came and went like a breeze.

"What happened to the book after you and your master found it?" I asked.

"Master Chiang stressed to me the danger of such books. He said they only existed because evil men who wished to expose secrets of the universe wrote them down. True magicians, he claimed, retained the knowledge inside them and did not need to transcribe it.

"He claimed to know a man in a nearby village who could safely dispose of such an object. I begged him not go, or at least to take me with him, but he refused. Our village could not be left without both its healers. And though I was still an apprentice, the people were my responsibly.

"He left that night, packing very few things and wrapping the book in cloth. I wept, for it seems I intuitively understood the danger. He took my hand, kissed the top of my head, told me I was his best pupil. Then he left into the night. I never saw him again. That's when the dreams started."

Dr. Li was quiet a long time. "The dreams..." he said finally, "followed me through college and all the way to the United States. I still have them sometimes. The same one, always the same. Your friend James is there, lying in a bed that's suspended in outer space. He looks very ill and wicked. He and I are speaking. Suddenly the sky shifts and I see this great, massive shape gliding through the cosmos sucking the planets and stars into itself, consuming them, digesting them. It's a horrifying vision, one I do not fully understand. When I awake, I am usually covered in sweat. Heart racing. I never want to go back to sleep after."

Annabelle refreshed his glass of diet soda and said, "When was the last time you had this dream?"

He thought. "Last week, I think. There are different variations but your sick friend and the silently moving being are always there."

He glanced to the ceiling, pointing, and added slyly, "And now they are both right here."

"Aren't we lucky," I joked.

He smiled. "We are, actually. This is an opportunity for karmic resolution. All of us are connected—our spirits are connected. I don't have to tell you that, do I, Roger? Not with your history and esoteric experiences."

It took me a second to realize he too was joking. I hardly recalled a thing about my occult past, so when I picked up the book, turning it over in my hands, I couldn't even remember how to decipher it.

"Can we use it?" I asked.

Dr. Li regarded the book. "Perhaps. Although it is preferable to destroy it."

"Destroy it? Why?"

"Master Chiang said it was an evil book, said that a true Taoist wizard would not need such a petty relic. I have my books. I have my needles. Unless you can think of another purpose for it."

"Well, I'm not a Taoist wizard. I'm a New Yorker. But actually, I have thought of another purpose."

"You have?"

I nodded. "Leverage."

They both displayed confusion.

"Allow me to explain. James seemed very proud of the fact that he had this book. He was reluctant to give it up. Who am I kidding? He fought me tooth and nail. I'm not sure if the Time Eater is attached to it, but I *am* sure James, the man lying up there sick, is attached to it. I believe he wants it back. Maybe we can use that."

Annabelle said, "Is that worth the danger of keeping it around?"

I considered. I'd traveled all the way into the city in search of it. That alone seemed like cause enough to keep it around—at least for me. But perhaps I was being selfish. Just because I thought the book was significant didn't mean it was. Still, I couldn't bring myself to destroy it.

"It's worth the danger," I said. My answer didn't seem to surprise them.

The next hour was spent discussing our plans for the evening. Dr. Li had several more items to prepare before we could go upstairs and begin. Annabelle agreed to help with that. He took some time to explain to us what he would be doing, but even after all that I felt I was in the dark about the procedure. But this I did understand: the doctor had his role to play; I had mine; and Annabelle had hers. And each role was very different.

* * *

By sundown, we were ready to begin. I had been pacing the living room for most of the evening, as Dr. Li and Annabelle readied the necessary ingredients. They'd really hit it off and made quite a natural team, I'd noticed. Now we were moving up the staircase, the doctor in the lead carrying his medical bag. I brought up the rear carrying a wooden dinner tray arranged with herbs, tonics, and other paraphernalia.

The house grew dark as we reached the second floor. Annabelle switched on the hallway light, its glare narrowing my eyes. "I have to use the bathroom before we start," she said.

"Me too," said the doctor.

"Great, I'll use the one in my bedroom and you can use the one in the hallway." She looked at me. "How 'bout you?"

"I'm fine. I think I'll just stand here holding this tray."

She smiled and then they both made their departures. I waited in the silence, listening for sounds coming from James's bedroom. I heard nothing, yet I imagined him sitting upright on the bed, eyes glowing in the dark, his head surrounded by stars.

Stop that, I told myself. *If you think of him as a demon, as some adversary, you'll never get through to him.*

I scoffed at my own words. The sound broke the silence and it was strange but I suddenly felt like I was totally alone in the house, talking to myself.

When they returned, I did my best to shake these feelings, without much success. *You're insane, this will never work*, I thought, realizing I was moments away from a panic attack.

Dr. Li had placed his hand on the doorknob. "Are we ready?"

Annabelle nodded. I took a deep breath, trying to calm my nerves. The doctor opened the door and we went in.

It was dark, as I'd imagine it would be. Annabelle tried the light switch but it appeared to malfunction. Thankfully, we had prepared for this, and after setting the tray down before the bed, the doctor lit three large white candles. The tiny flames shattered the room into a broken window of light and dark.

James was lying in bed, facing the wall. He had the sheet pulled over him. His body was so thin, so emaciated, that for a moment I couldn't distinguish between him and the wrinkles in the bedding.

"Jesus, he looks like shit," I whispered.

The doctor held a finger to his lips and shook his head at me. Annabelle scooted a small end table over by the bed, placing the tray on it. They lit a few more candles and Annabelle placed them around the room. She set one in the bathroom. The walls, the piles of old clothing, board games and assorted junk, and the heavy drapes overhanging the window—all of it seemed to fade in the flickering candlelight. It began to resemble, at least to my mind, the interior of some old Gothic castle, torches gutting, walls made of interconnected stones. The veil of reality trembled... and I knew we had begun.

Annabelle opened the folding chair she had brought from

downstairs and sat, while Dr. Li assumed position in the single wood chair. It looked like I would have to stand or sit on the floor.

James began stirring. As soon as he rolled over the roof overhead evaporated, replaced by a canopy of stars. He shook himself to banish the drowsiness and sat up. He looked like hell, face sunken, hair a mess, bags under his eyes. He sat watching us without saying a word.

The doctor handed me one of the tonics they had prepared in a plastic cup. "He must drink this," he said.

I realized he was telling me James might refuse the drink, that it was up to me to work this out. I sighed, took the tonic, stepped to the bed.

Without turning, James flicked his eyes to me. He watched me intently, a cat eying a ball of yarn. When I extended the plastic cup to him, he suddenly sprang to life, batting at it with both hands. I quickly drew it back.

"The hell's your problem?" I said, loudly because the sudden movement had startled me. "You have to drink it, James. No way around it."

He scowled. "Why should I?"

"Because it'll relax you and we need you to be relaxed while we..." I was going to lay it all out for him—the procedure Dr. Li had in store, the acupuncture needles, the herb tonics—but without meaning to I glanced at the doctor, who gave me his sharpest look.

Then something crazy happened, something that wasn't possible in normal reality and could only happen here at the threshold of the veil. I heard his voice inside my head, clear as a bell.

Lie to him. Tell him what he wants to hear. Don't try and reach him, he's beyond that. The only way is the way of deception.

I gave a nod, then shook my head as if to dispel Dr. Li's voice. It took me less than a second to figure out what to tell James.

"Nurse Norma has been by," I said.

His eyes widened. "She has?"

"Yep. And she dropped off your medicine."

At this point, I noticed his facial features undergoing a terrible change. His forehead and cheekbones slanted forward, becoming more angular, and he altogether appeared sharper around the edges. He had become that rodent-thing again. When he spoke, his words came out in a hiss.

"You mean the morphine, don't you? But I thought... Why did

she not come up to see me?"

"She was afraid you were mad at her."

His mouth fell open. "Me, mad at her? What for?"

"Because she stopped coming around, stopped giving you your medication."

He became sullen. "Actually, I am mad about that."

"Well, have no fear. She has left the responsibility to yours truly. But because it's been a few days since your last dose, she advised me to give you this."

I proffered the cup, but he wrinkled his nose at it. "Why would I need that?"

"Your body is in detox. If we gave you the morphine, there's a chance it might send you into a panic. If you drink this first it will help calm you. It's only a mild sedative."

I was lying my ass off, but I held the cup out again, playing it cool. I could tell he was having trouble believing me. However, the thought of getting high again was so influential that he was willing to believe anything.

He took the cup and drank it, cringed, and spit out something that resembled watermelon seeds. "What the hell is this—" he started to say, then instantly fell onto his side, snoring.

I lifted one of his arms, dropped it, and it landed limply beside him. "Some powerful shit," I said.

Dr. Li was pleased. "You did well, Roger. People in his position have trouble remembering they want to live. The allure of death becomes too great, and they must be swayed back to the light with extreme care. Lay him on his back and remove his shirt."

I did, flopping James over. His body felt like rolled up carpeting: clumsy, hard to manage. I got him into the position Dr. Li wanted, his head on the pillow, limbs splayed, and shirtless.

I returned to Annabelle, placing my hand on her shoulder. She placed hers on top of it, smiling at me.

"How you feeling?" I asked.

"On edge. I hope everything works out."

I squeezed her hand. "Me too."

We watched the doctor work. First he checked James's tongue, then his pulse, remarking to us that in Chinese medicine there were three different pulses: *Chu, Guan,* and *Chi,* positioned in three places along the wrists. He applied strange ointments to James's chest, fragrant balms he and Annabelle had prepared over the last few hours. One after another, layer after layer, they all were applied, until the intoxicating mixture of scents pervaded the room. My head began to swim with smells.

Dr. Li signaled for my assistance and together we rolled James onto his stomach. I recoiled from the sight of his back, which was discolored by rashes.

"Bedsores?" I asked.

He didn't answer, but shooed me away. I returned to Annabelle. "He doesn't look well," she said.

The doctor opened a wooden box on the tray. Inside was an arrangement of small glass cups. He moved over to the bed with the box and one of the candles. "Now, we will draw the physical toxins out. Body first, mind second."

He heated up the inside of each cup with the flame before attaching it, with suction, to James's back. He used every cup in the box—twelve in all. James's back was covered with them.

The doctor returned to his seat, sighing heavily. "Twenty-minute wait now."

"The heat draws the toxins into the cups, right?" Annabelle said.

Dr. Li nodded, closing his eyes to rest. We waited.

I went to my knees beside Annabelle and placed my head on her lap. She stroked my hair. *I love her*, I was thinking. *I can't believe I'm actually in love again.*

As we sat there quietly, allowing the cupping method to run its course, the room began to darken around the candlelight. Being absorbed in my thoughts, I didn't notice—until Annabelle abruptly sucked in a breath.

I opened my eyes. "What?"

"It's coming."

I jerked my head up. Both Annabelle and Dr. Li were watching the space of wall opposite the bed. The darkness, which was filling the room like a vast black fog, seemed to be coming from that spot. I was reminded of the smoke machines used at rock concerts.

The doctor stood. For a moment he was silhouetted against a backdrop of dark and empty space. I felt queasy looking at him, as though I were gazing down from a very tall building.

"What will we do when the Time Eater comes?" I asked.

He glanced at me on his way to the bed. "We will deal with it."

One by one, he began removing the cups and placing them back in the box. Wherever there had been one, a red ring remained visible on James's skin. It looked like he'd been branded with a circular metal rod. To my amazement, the rashes on his back had cleared up.

On cue, I assisted the doctor in flipping James onto his back. His whole complexion had improved and some of the color had returned to his face.

"Now what?"

To Annabelle, he said, "Bring the bag of stones."

She retrieved a cloth drawstring bag from the tray and ferried it over to the doctor. He opened it, spilling the contents into his palm. A collection of polished stones varying in color and shape gleamed in the candlelight.

He began placing these at various points on James's body: crown of his head, forehead, throat, heart, stomach, two at his groin. "The chakras," he told us briefly.

Annabelle retrieved his set of acupuncture needles, which he placed on the bed beside James. We returned to the chairs, allowing Dr. Li space to work. He had his large leather book opened to a page full of diagrams indicating various points on the human body. He consulted the book frequently.

This reminded me of my own special book, the one we had used to summon the Time Eater. I touched its hard cover through the fabric of my jacket pocket, where I had placed it. I wasn't sure what I was going to do with it yet. All I knew was that I couldn't give it up.

For several minutes, we watched Dr. Li applying his needles. I grew fascinated with his method. My only previous exposure to acupuncture was during my trip to China with Jenny, and that had been marginal. Now I was getting a firsthand experience.

The needles weren't jabbed into the flesh, as my provincial mind had imagined. Instead he used insertion tubes, little plastic cylinders that the needles fit into. He would find the correct acupuncture point with his finger, place the tube against his skin with the needle inside, and give it a quick tap. Afterward, he retracted the tube, leaving the freestanding needle in place.

The process was repeated manifold, as the doctor created a vast web of interconnecting needles all along James's body. Dr. Li worked with expertise, care, and finesse. I was altogether spellbound by his movements. He seemed lost to his own thoughts, either that or connected to a higher power, a power that guided his hands.

By the time he finished, Annabelle and I were leaning forward on the edge of our chairs, staring at Dr. Li's small body as he went up and down James's torso and limbs, inserting needles. He finally reached the head and face, using great care locating the exact point—under the eyes, one between both eyes, around his neck, the top of his head, carefully avoiding the chakra stones.

Meanwhile, the darkness coming from the spot in the wall filled the room until nothing but black empty space surrounded us. Toward the end of the procedure, as the stars and planets began to come out, I realized we were no longer alone, that the Time Eater had finally arrived. I could sense it—I believed all of us could—lurking behind everything, like a television left on with no one around. I kept waiting for it to rear its ugly amoebic form, but so far it lurked in the shadows.

The doctor straightened, moving from the bed, and gazed down at his work. He stroked his long beard, brows knit. He consulted his book once more, then said, "I've directed his qi through a specific course, guiding it up toward his mind, and now there is only one point left before the procedure is complete."

"What are you waiting for?" I said. "The Time Eater could come at us at any moment."

The doctor frowned. "I don't know. I suppose I'm scared. I've never taken the procedure so far before. This point—this final point— is an esoteric one. Few know of it at all. I only know because of my master. Once inserted, I'm not exactly sure what will happen. But the pattern will be finished."

"What can you predict?" Annabelle asked.

"I predict it will cure him, that it will get rid of the illness and the presence of the Time Eater. In my dreams…"

He became absorbed in his thoughts. In fact, he seemed tortured by worry, as though desperately trying to figure something out. Finally he said, "In my dreams, nothing is resolved. I never get to see the end."

"Only one way to find out," I said.

He smiled. "You are right. There is only one way."

"Where is the secret point?" Annabelle asked.

Dr. Li took a fresh needle and approached the bed. He leaned over James's head. "It is right…"

Suddenly James shot up, sending all the chakra stones flying. Dr.

Li was propelled off his feet, stumbling back with a crash. The needle went plummeting from his hand.

"Li!" Annabelle cried, rushing over.

My attention latched to the sight of James, filled with needles, sitting up in bed. He was leering at me, face like a rabid animal, eyes wide and filled with intensity. The needles covering his body, like a coat of spiny fur, glimmered and twinkled.

"You lied to me, Roger," he said.

I jumped to my feet. "James, I—"

He blew me off with a wave of his hand. "Don't give me your excuses, man. I'm not as dumb as you think I am. Just because I didn't spend my youth with my nose in a book like you doesn't mean I don't know anything. I know plenty. I know you said you were going to give me my medicine and instead I get this—more pain."

He held his arms out, the needles running all along them. For a moment he resembled the crucified Jesus from my earlier vision. Seeing him in this state filled me with sympathy and guilt. *My God*, I thought, *what have I done to him?*

"James, I'm sorry. You said you wanted to live, you told me that—"

"What I want," he said, raising his voice, "is to have my fucking medicine *now!*"

The energy in the room darkened to match James's emotions. There was a sound like white noise or static. I sensed movement—massive movement—gliding soundlessly overhead, behind us, beneath us, everywhere.

The Time Eater had come.

Wind. A sucking, pulling wind, snatching my clothes, my hair, and the corners of the bed sheets. In the remote distance, stars and planets and other cosmic phenomena were drawn toward something unseen, lurking beyond the limits of perception.

James's rat-like face split into a grin. "You won't give me what I want, I know something else that will," he said. A beam of swirling light suddenly shone from above, pinpointing James like a spotlight. He arched his back, sticking his chest out. He didn't seem to be accomplishing this feat of his own free will. It was like something was pulling him, had lassoed him around the waist, tightened the rope, now tugging. His head thrust backward, eyes rolling, torso bulging out unnaturally. The myriad needles shimmered.

"Christ, James!" I said, rushing to the bed. The moment my knees touched down on the mattress, the spotlight grew brighter, so bright I had to shield my eyes. I lost sight of James, the room, the world. The only thing visible was the bouquet of acupuncture needles gouged into his skin.

As the light dimmed, pooled, then petered away, he collapsed to his knees, looking like a martyr in supplication. To my horror I saw the needles were gone. They'd changed somehow into hypodermic syringes, filled with a clear fluid I knew was morphine.

He rose, a tattered angel, limp arms hanging like wings. But he grinned, the wickedest, most vile grin I had ever seen. It put fear into my heart. The syringes dangled, spiny tips bending, thumb plungers depressing of their own accord. All at once, the barrels began to empty, flooding James's bloodstream with a god-awful amount of narcotics.

"Yes..." he said. The word whistled through his clenched teeth. "That is what I needed, *yes*..."

His body began to shiver. All at once his skin flushed. When the barrels were empty, the syringes hung limply, clinging to the spoiled flesh. James sagged, bloodshot eyes awash with confusion and disorientation.

"Goddam you!" I screamed at the surrounding dark. "We are gonna get rid of you, we're gonna send you to Hell!"

There was a rumble of thunder from the empty abyss hanging above us. James shook on the mattress, writhing in drug-induced ecstasy. Seeing him that way made me feel ill, hopeless, defeated.

Searching for Annabelle and Dr. Li, my eyes lifted, scanning. In the distant black depths beyond the bed, where the stars and the colorful space clouds were being sucked away, I saw it. Coming from the space in the wall, now far-off, nearly imperceptible, but coming...

The sight of it effectively threw off my perception of size. I was five foot eleven and the hole in the wall was a mere three inches, but the Time Eater was as immense as an entire planet, huge and vast and trundling. The only reason I saw it in its entirety was because it was far away in the distance, like looking through a telescope. But in reality, it was only several feet away.

It came crawling out of the bottomless pit at the other end of the room. Colossal, shaped like an inkblot, screaming and warbling. A massive patch housed in a purple membranous wall, moving like an underwater creature, a pulsating jellyfish, splitting apart at times, then merging back together. I saw grand and terrible visions of alien landscapes, but I couldn't be certain because overall I saw blackness. I was disoriented, and I thought, perhaps, I was shrinking.

The wind picked up, tugging silently. On the bed James was turned onto his side. I wanted to go to him, help him, pull one of those horrific syringes out—something—but I remained paralyzed in the presence of the Time Eater.

I watched in horror as James was nearly stripped off the bed. But at the last instant Dr. Li emerged from the dark with Annabelle in tow. He wore his fiercest, most intense expression. He tugged at his beard, showing his tiny square teeth.

One hand raised, I saw he was wielding his acupuncture needle like a slasher's blade. He slid right up behind James, grabbed him by the shoulders and pressed the needle against the side of his head—his left temple. With a lightning-quick flick of his wrist, he implanted the needle in the flesh, casting the insertion tube away.

A look of serenity entered the doctor's face the moment before he went down, collapsing into a heap. He looked me right in the eyes and mouthed the word, *You.*

I didn't understand, so I shook my head, but I could tell he was overjoyed and endlessly pleased with himself. He'd done it. He'd completed the procedure and finished the pattern. After he fell over Annabelle followed after him, making sure he was all right.

Left alone in the darkness, the wind whipping into a frenzy, threatening to swipe me off my feet. I tried to make sense of what was happening. James floated off the bed like a puppet, held aloft by unseen strings. The moment Dr. Li put the last needle into him, he came apart with light, splitting like a fractured stained glass window. Now he appeared *unwhole*, a disassembled jigsaw puzzle of himself, spewing light in all directions, a human chandelier. I clenched my breath against the sheer awesomeness of it.

His body started to rotate, round and round, sending out light beams, penetrating the dark. Beyond him, bulbous and jittering overhead, the Time Eater descended with tremendous speed.

Finally, we were fighting back.

I wanted to grab James, pull him down, but the moment I got too close, the Time Eater lurched forward. It seemed to come out of nowhere, falling down, around, on top of me, the bed, the whole room. The wind was a tempest, blowing in all directions. For one horrible moment, I could see the being suspended over me; its vast warbling body became the sky, its imperceptible wailing filled the air.

It swallowed us, I thought. *We're inside it now, dead, dying, being digested. It's won. It's removed us from time—*

—but my attention was drawn back to James's spinning, hovering body. Shafts of light fell outward through cracks in his skin, as he spun and spun and spun. The syringes had turned back into needles, and I happened to catch a glimpse of his face flying by and nearly had a heart attack.

No. Impossible. Can't be—

Frozen, I waited for him to come back around, my gaze fixed firmly in place. The wind and the vast shape of the Time Eater threatened to divert me, but I held fast—I had to see. I had to know.

Had it been…

All along…

Here it comes…

I watched, hoping I was mistaken. But as he whirled toward me I looked into his face. It was not James. Not his eyes, cheeks, nose, or mouth, not his hair. It happened in slow motion, the moment becoming eternity, and I suddenly understood, suddenly recognized the awful truth.

The weight of it was crushing. My knees fell apart and I thought I would collapse. James (*who the hell is James?*) went whirling back, taking his horrible truth with him. His secret. Light spilled forth, engulfing the room, as I recalled what Dr. Li had said to me, his last and final word before going down—

You.

Me, had he meant me?

This is all a dream, I told myself. *Any moment you are going to wake up back in your apartment, still alone, still divorced, still bitter, the way it's always been.*

I couldn't believe that, no, I had to fight that kind of thinking. What I'd seen, what I had recognized in James's passing face, must have been a trick, a deception on the part of the Time Eater. I couldn't allow myself to believe it; to believe was to surely go insane.

The Time Eater, encompassing everything in sight, trembled and wailed. The purple membrane that housed it shone brighter so that the corners of every direction were a purple band. Up above, the terrible blackness reached.

And it was coming fast…

Stars, planets, and drifting clouds of space-dust were obliterated in its stygian depths. I saw them as in a vision being grinded soundlessly apart, without effort, simply dematerializing. I'm not sure what it was about seeing this that struck me. As I watched the cosmic phenomena, I became aware that everything in the room was dissolving. Everything was floating away: piles of junk and clothes hauled up by the wind, curtains, walls, doors, the tray of Dr. Li's paraphernalia, everything collapsing like cardboard cutouts.

The bed was pulled down through the floor, which had become a yawning pit. James, too, left to hover and rotate a moment longer, was flicked as by some unseen finger to pinwheel off in the darkness where the Time Eater got him, absorbed him.

I stood in emptiness and it became too much, the wind became too strong, and then I was overwhelmed and started falling. The last thing I saw on my way to oblivion was my dear, sweet Annabelle being taken from me. Arms outstretched, she beckoned, but I was already on my way out.

I could see the message she was trying to impart, the final offering escaping mutely from her lips, words fueled by power and meaning.

I love you too, Roger, she said.

Then I was ashes.

Chapter Nineteen

We have a feeling in childhood that vanishes after puberty—or, if it doesn't vanish, then it remains in a much smaller distribution. This feeling is green, broad, and magical. We are born with a superabundance of this stuff, but we lose it by degrees as we grow older, as we learn about the world in which we live. We adapt to the pressures of our parents, teachers, religious advisors, friends, until this feeling gets snubbed out and we are left hollow, angry, alone.

My mother died on the day I was born. Complications from the direction I was facing. I also heard rumors of hemorrhaging. I never got a straight answer from my father about it. He'd always placated my questioning, explaining to me—rather cynically—that it must've been God's will.

But my mother's brother—Uncle Dennis—he was there that day. Although he's dead now too, I got to ask him my questions before he died. He told me that after an excruciating couple of hours, during which the doctors and nurses worked to get me delivered, I was finally liberated, umbilicus cut, and placed on my mother's soft, taut belly. This moment of skin-to-skin contact lasted five seconds. Then machines started beeping, doctors started shouting. Ripped from my mother's body, I was handed to a nurse. I never felt my mother's touch again. Five seconds: that's all I got.

Strangely, I've retained fragmentary images of this event, lodged in the depths of my unconscious, and yet surfacing once in a while in my dreams. I see myself going down the hall in the nurse's arms. I see the lights and the long clear windows. I experience the horrible detachment I felt being taken away from her. I had experienced my mother's warm skin, her safety, her nurturing presence, and then just as suddenly, snatched away and cold again, clutched in someone's rubbery-gloved hands.

It's here that I feel myself split. Part of me wanted to be back with her so badly—as if I knew intuitively she was dying and would never get another chance—that this part willed itself back to her, or at least tried to. Who knows how far it got. Would anyone have noticed shattered fragments of a newborn baby's psyche floating through the air to its mother? Not likely.

Still, that's what I see: part of me straining back to return to the delivery room, and the other part being ferried away. Accompanying these images is a feeling of extreme terror and rage that I can only re-experience at half the intensity. Re-experiencing it fully would break me down in tears or leave me suicidal. Beyond this, any thoughts and images of my birth and my mother end.

Then comes a sinking feeling, especially since I was to be around my father all the time. I don't think he ever reconciled my mother's death. He never remarried—a telling sign. He couldn't be affectionate with me because to look into my eyes was to see his own grief mirrored back at him. So there we were, two human males lost in a world where the woman in their lives had been taken.

This was the sad, unloving environment I was raised in.

Unable to cope, and overcome by work, my father hired a live-in midwife named Sandy. Sandy was an attractive young woman who spent copious hours with me, even breastfed me. I believe it's safe to say that despite her attractive appearance and nurturing capability, my father never slept with her. No, by then he'd already given up completely.

As I grew older, Sandy was replaced by a series of babysitters. Most were either teenage girls or incredibly gray-looking women. I don't have many memories of them or of building any significant bonds. I do, however, get glimpses of my father from this time. I can see him, tall and gaunt, dressed in his work clothes, sitting at the kitchen table reading the paper or in front of the TV, drinking Italian beer. The impression I get is one of deep guilt and sadness.

We lived in Upstate New York, in the house where my mother and father conceived me. Even after she died, my father refused to get rid of her things. It wasn't until I went off to college at Ohio State that he finally consented, transferring the bulk of her wardrobe to a spare bedroom.

When that time came, I couldn't get out the door and on the

airplane fast enough. The world I'd lived in had been perpetually shrinking and the confining atmosphere was beginning to drive me stir crazy. I've suspected that I was the last anchor holding my father back from the edge, and so after I left the rest of the world closed in on him, and he died not long after. I didn't attend his funeral.

What I remember most about those years in Upstate New York, aside from my father's endless moping and my string of indifferent babysitters, were the woods. In the backyard, out past the deck and the grassy plot dotted with towering maples and a few unused hammocks, stretched a deep forested area that reached all the way back to a flowing stream. This became my saving grace, my habitual playground.

At a young age, probably around six, I started wandering off into the woods behind our home. My father, a constant recluse, encouraged this activity, but he told me never to venture beyond the stream. A stone-lined path cut through the maze of gnarled trunks, and as long as I stuck to that, he said, I'd be fine.

I experienced overwhelming emotions of fear and abandonment, which arrived suddenly without external cause. Thanks to the years I spent married to Jenny—and all the talking we did—I recognized these feelings later as maternal depravation. I never had a mother; instinctively, I knew I was *supposed* to have one; *and*, on an intuitive level, I knew that by being born I had in fact killed my mother.

So, according to Jenny (whom I for one believed), the feeling of loss was based on the belief that she'd abandoned me because I'd somehow been bad, failed her. Having been bad, I deserved to be punished, and that punishment was coming... I just didn't know when.

As a child, whenever these emotions came on I liked to escape into the woods, into a world of magic. I left my other self, the normal kid living a normal life, and embraced another part of me, a part less distinctive, more fluid, a part possessing greater spiritual inheritance.

In the woods, I could experience this part with all of my being. Since the reducing and contaminative elements of the adult world had not yet set in, my imagination was alive. The trees were angels, every blade of grass was a star, and the ferns and other red shrubs were living creatures of wonder and awe. The branches reached their leafy limbs above me, creating security, while underfoot stretched a floor of silken dirt.

These woods were my hideaway from the grief of my father, the babysitters and cleaning women, from the schools I attended where I felt disdained by other students, away from ordinary life, immersing myself in a world I had created.

It's impossible to say how much time I spent in the wooded arms of that wonderland. I do remember how much I loved the stream at the end of the path. Crystal as a clear sky in summer, its waters came swirling out of the upper regions of the Adirondacks to go trickling over a bed of jeweled rocks. I would often sit by the shore listening to its babbling song, a gurgling concerto filling the air. I imagined it was playing just for me. In this world of magic I'd created for my other self, all things knew me and loved me and worshiped me. They were all my friends, and I was never alone.

(Here's where my memories become patchy, only... now I seem to be recovering —)

I recall sitting by the stream one day—Christ, I must have been eight years old—listening and watching the sunlight reflecting in the water. I was selecting flat stones from along the bank, skipping them across the surface.

A man emerged out of the trees on my left. Was it a man? I felt unsure. I was frightened because I thought it was an animal, a wolf, a stag, or a black bear. But when I looked up from the little pile of flat stones I'd been assembling, I saw it was a man. He stood there, thin, angular, wearing tattered blue overalls, brown boots, and a straw hat.

When he noticed me, he stopped. I saw he had a long thin weed hanging over his bottom lip, which he chewed. Behind those lips... teeth black and crooked and slightly bared. Eyes like two lumps of coal set into fresh bread dough. I remember that put me off more than anything—the horror of his eyes—because it was like looking at a dead person.

He waved to me. I waved back. He had an old-fashioned fishing rod slung over one shoulder, a yellow tackle box clutched in his other hand. He kept looking around like he was expecting someone. But no one came. After a few minutes of searching for a suitable place to set his line, he came over to where I was sitting.

"Howdy," he said.

I remember looking up at him, how it felt like looking at a giant. The sky, crisscrossed by branches, reared behind his head, endless. The shape of his hat, and the shadow it cast across his face, seemed larger than life. It was like the magic of the woods had given birth to this towering figure.

"Hello," I said.

He glanced at my rock pile. "What's that you got?"

"Some rocks. I like to skip them across the stream."

He chuckled. "Yes, I do that sometimes. Mind if I join yah? I think this'll be a good spot to get a nibble."

I shrugged my shoulders. He set his tackle box down in the dirt.

We remained quiet for a while. He set his pole in the water and watched it sink to the bottom. The rushing stream closed over it, parting around the line and forming rippling currents. His pole was not like the ones I'd seen other people fishing with: metal, with a crank to turn the reel. His was nothing but a stick with some fishing line attached to it. I remember thinking that was weird. I couldn't imagine why he'd chosen that sort of a rod over the more convenient types.

I asked him about it, and he glanced at me sidelong without responding. He did this frequently, kind of peeked at me, watching. I got annoyed. Here I was minding my own business, when this weird guy waltzes over and doesn't even say anything, just watches me, like I was a TV show or something. I didn't like it.

Finally he said, "You only need a pole of this caliber for pulling trout out of a stream this small. Fly fishing also works. It's when you're fishing in a lake or the sea that you need the type of pole you're talking about."

He looked at me, and I nodded without fully understanding. Then he said, "Say, what are you doing out here all a-by yourself? Don't you have school, parents?"

"We're on break," I said. "My mom's dead, and my dad… don't care much what I do or where I am."

He made a noise in his throat. "A dead mother, an indifferent father… that's a shame. Christ, I'm sorry, boy."

He'd said he was sorry, and I remember thinking there was nothing to be sorry about, but in his face he displayed another emotion. His cheeks cracked in a leering rictus, a smile too wide and too broad to be anything but grotesque. A gleam twinkled in his eyes, dancing around those leaden black eyebrows. He peered into the forest the way he had come, muttering, "…a real shame."

(God, no. No, no honestly, no really—that? Is that what happened, are you sure, are you positive? Oh God! Why—?)

The man returned to watching his fishing pole, but something about the scene was now different. I felt a heavy weight hanging over us, a thing encumbering but unseen, holding back the blue sky, invisible. He was looking both at me and over his shoulder, one way then the other, a series of quick, feverish neck-swivels like a deranged animal. It frightened me.

That heavy unseen presence lingered. For a moment, I thought I saw a great shadow fall upon the stream, a dark amorphous shape stretching over the water.

"You sure ain't nobody missing you right now?" he said, and again I noticed that horrible eagerness and excitement in his voice, present just beneath the words. He began doing something with his free hand—something having to do with the straps of his overalls. But my mind was too preoccupied with that unseen shape, the roiling blackness hovering like a swarm of bees over the water.

It lurched then—all of it: the blackness, the shadow, the stream, the trees, the man. It all rocked to one side, then settled back into position. An explosion of sights and sounds entered into my field of vision. I heard ringing. I saw colorful starbursts wheeling over the water. A crack had opened, shaped like a lightning bolt, above the stream, directly in the center of the blackness.

Through the crack passed something old and silent and massive, something full of dead stars and digested planets, something warbling in its own purple vacuum, something beyond my wildest dreams.

Then the pain hit. I realized that my head was banging and my ears were ringing. My teeth had chomped down on my tongue and I tasted blood. I looked up toward the man who was standing over me. In his right hand, he held one of the boots he'd taken off, was holding it above his head.

I touched my head, felt warm liquid. Looked at my hands. It was blood. "You… you hit me."

"Uh-huh," he said maniacally. "That ain't all I'm gonna do…"

His hand came down like a hawk out of the sky. A curled and twisted claw trying to close around my neck. I batted it away, but he kept thrusting it at me. Soon both of his claws were out and reaching. No matter what, he wouldn't stop.

"Leave me alone!" I shouted, struggling to my feet. But the second I attempted to move, the world and all its stars danced again. The blood leaked down into my eyes and I grew nauseous, tumbling back in the dirt. The man pounced on me, throwing all his weight on top of me. I screamed.

"Shut your rotten mouth or I'll kill you!" he snarled. His boot came down and knocked the world off kilter. I tasted bile. I sensed darkness closing in on my periphery. A dropping sensation—down and down—but where was I going? Was I about to die?

He flipped me on my stomach, and then the weirdest thing—my pants were stripped down, along with my underwear, allowing the cool forest air to tickle my skin. I was overwhelmed by confusion. Nothing made sense.

He lied down on top of me, crushing me with his weight. I suddenly noticed he too had his underwear down, though I couldn't imagine why. My eyes looked out across the tranquil stream, over which hung that indescribable darkness, ancient and lurking behind it all, seeable but unseen. A wind, rustling the trees, flung leaves on the surface of the water.

"I'm gonna split you good, boy," he breathed into my ear. "Split you right in the middle."

An explosion of pain. Pressure, assault, violent tearing.

I screamed again.

"Shut your mouth!" he cried. "Do as your daddy says and it'll be over afore you know it!"

His hand covered my mouth. I thought about biting it, but suddenly a wave of vomit rose in my throat. The violent throttling I experienced caused me to swallow the vomit down inadvertently, and I started choking. My vision dimmed.

I imagined I was a fish, like the darting trout I had glimpsed in the stream. Only I was dead and being dashed against a rock by some wild boar. But what did I care? Dead things didn't feel pain. They didn't get confused or scared. Dead things just lied there.

So that's what I did. And as I lied there, my eyes zeroed in on the black shape over the stream. It seemed to be opening itself like a flower. It grew larger, wider, stranger, darker, and deep in its depths I glimpsed stars being pulverized, whole planets being rent to dust. I was mesmerized and somehow the amazement managed to block out the pain. For that I was glad.

All at once, the shape reached out to me. Distorted purple appendages made of light and stardust. Warm, comforting, like saviors sent to bear me away from this torture. I wanted to fling myself into them, into those two purplish limbs stretching across the stream. But I was pinned, my whole body crushed under the weight of a wild boar.

So I sent my other self. The one that existed before my mother's death and my father's mourning had distorted it. I gave up the part of me that loved magic, the woods, the world. I thought by doing so, I could save it. I thought the blooming black being would carry it away.

However, the moment I sent it out, the being changed. It turned into a hungry ravenous beast—hungrier than the man on top of me— and it sent out a violent wind to suck me up, pull my other self into its depths.

I felt that part of me go. And after it left I felt empty and exposed and alone. I suddenly understood I'd made a grievous mistake. The black being, now shrinking into the background, disappearing into the trees, was not my savior. It was my captor. It had tricked me, and now it had the most precious part of me—my other self, the magic self— and I knew it would never, under any circumstances, give it back. Not unless it was forced to.

It had me, and now it was gone, back from whence it came. I was left lying by the bank of the stream, trapped under a monster who was inflicting the greatest suffering on me. The feeling of falling returned and darkness filled my eyes. The world went black and I realized, at that moment, I would never be the same.

Chapter Twenty

(Now I know. Now I know what you wanted me to forget. And now that I know, I swear—I swear to that part of me which is magic, which is holy—I will never forget again.)

Chapter Twenty-One

Light. Coming from all corners, closing in, circulating. It came from above like rain, from below like waves, from both sides, where it entered my vision like a pair of collapsing walls. Soon it was everywhere—in everything. Then, as it began to dim, I saw shapes.

The last thing I could remember was the horror of lying beside the stream. The horror of what that awful man did to me.

But I wasn't in the forest. I was in a dark room whose windows had been thrown open, through which spilled great yellow shafts of sunlight. Piles of clothes and rags, furniture covered in sheets, and stacks of old board games surrounded me. A group of people I didn't recognize sat close by.

"Look. He's up," one of them said. The voice was female.

I found that I was, in fact, lying down, but not on the ground beside the stream. I was in a large wooden bed without a blanket, my lower half wrapped in a sheet. I was shirtless. My body felt incredibly weary. To move an inch seemed like the greatest task, and so I just stayed still, and that felt good.

Slowly the room came into focus, including the people sitting around me. The clearer I saw them, the more I began to remember. But it was confusing. I scanned their faces. The small Chinese man with gray hair and a beard, with a face like an angel's. I remembered him. He was the acupuncturist. Someone (was it me?) had gone into the city to contact him. Next to him stood a small table with a number of strange-looking Asian items scattered across it: candles, scrolls with Chinese characters, smoking sticks resembling incense, curious glass cups, and a slew of acupuncture needles. I could still feel the pinpricks all over my body and the hot bruises on my back from where the cupping had been performed.

In the chair beside the small doctor sat Annabelle. Her face was a vision, her long black hair falling around her shoulders. She had tears on her cheeks, messing up her mascara.

"How do you feel?" she asked.

"Great. A bit tired. Actually I feel like I could sleep a week, but other than that... yeah, great."

She smiled as more tears came, then reached forward to touch my arm. But my attention had turned to the people standing behind Annabelle and the doctor. I was speechless, in shock. I stared at them wide-eyed, my mouth hanging open.

"Bet you haven't been mind-fucked like that since you were married to me," said Jenny, giving me a wink. She looked exactly as I remembered, yet slightly older and more dignified. She was every bit as attractive, her face a mask of perfectly drawn make up, her eyes crystal blue, framed in straight blonde hair.

I couldn't answer her, couldn't get my tongue to function, so my eyes strayed to the woman next to Jenny. Celeste. She too looked as I remembered, not a young college co-ed, but a pretty middle-aged brunette woman about my age. At that instant I was flooded with memories. Who the hell was she? And how did I—

"Didn't think you'd get rid of me that easy, did you?" she said, smirking.

My brain felt like it was going through convulsions. Nothing made sense. I was all mixed up. When I saw the final person standing by the bed—Norma, the woman who'd been my—I mean James's—nurse, I was overwhelmed. My memories and my awareness of time crumbled.

"What the fuck is going on?" I said. "How the hell did you all get here?"

"Drink this," Dr. Li said, handing me a tonic, "and take these," a handful of various herb pills. "That will stimulate memory as well as relaxation."

I swallowed the pills, dousing them in tonic. Everything had an acrid taste, but I managed to keep it down. I felt the effects almost instantly.

"How do you feel, James?" the doctor asked.

I chuckled sleepily. "Who are you calling James? What are you talking about, my name is Roger Borough—"

"Christ, you guys weren't kidding," Jenny interrupted. "I had no idea it had gotten this bad. I mean, when we were married there were signs, but he never—"

"When we were married," Celeste said, "I sometimes caught him signing his bills as Roger Borough. The times when I didn't catch him, of course, they came right back."

"What's this?" I said. I felt too dopey to fully comprehend their words, however I was conscious of a low murmuring in my skull, an underlying suspicion. An image floated into the blackness behind my eyelids: an inflated rubber ball rising up through the water.

The doctor leaned forward, bringing his massive gray face up close. "Your name isn't Roger Borough. Roger Borough is a delusion, an alternate personality you created in your head following the incident with the man beside the stream, the man who raped you."

"That's crazy. What the hell are you telling me, that I'm..." But I couldn't even finish the sentence, for I was overcome by a vast, black, paralyzing fear. Anxiety flooded my blood.

"*Christ, what's going on?*" I screamed into the doctor's calm, emotionless face.

He sighed. "This is all part of the process, James. Your whole entire life you have hid from this memory, denied it to yourself—and with good reason. The man by the stream told you he'd kill you if you ever told anyone what he did. Being a child, you believed him. However, this forced you to turn the pain inward. You repressed it, and that repressed part of you split away, became Roger Borough. All along you remained James Steiner. Although James was the more dominant, the two personalities existed inside you simultaneously.

"You presented yourself as either one depending on how you were feeling. When you were in high school, you did this to some extent, but it wasn't until you went to Ohio State and got away from your father that the spilt-personality *really* turned on. In college you consistently displayed yourself as two separate people: one who was a sports-playing jock, the other an occultist bookworm. In a sense, you led two different lives. It's a good thing Ohio State is so big or else you might have attracted more attention than you already did. You weren't able to fool everyone concerning your two lives, and so you gained a reputation of being eccentric. This, in combination with all the magic spells you were casting for people, made you a... how do you say it in English—*ominous* figure?"

I was flabbergasted. I stared at him with my face full of awe. The worst part was that somewhere deep inside, I knew everything he'd said was true. It was only a matter of letting myself accept it.

"How do you know all that?" I asked him, a tinge of anger in my voice.

Jenny answered. "Dr. Li interviewed us after Annabelle called to inform us of your condition. The rest *you* actually told him, laying right there in that bed, and he filled us in once we got here."

I looked to Annabelle, who was crying. "You called them?" She nodded. Then I felt compelled to ask, "What does this mean for us?" She started to answer, but I cut in—"No wait, I know. You and I were next-door neighbors back when I lived with my father... back before that man did what he did with me. We hung out sometimes, played doctor, all that. Is that right? I'm pretty sure we liked each other— boyfriend and girlfriend liked—but, by the time we became old enough to understand, we were too good of friends to wanna risk it?"

She nodded, crying, and took my hand. "You've basically got it. Although you forgot one thing."

"I did?"

"We also shared our first kiss together, one day in fifth grade, during recess. It was be—"

"—hind the bleachers on the softball field," I finished. "I do remember. You were so special, tolerating me even when I acted like a crazy weirdo. But..."

I looked at all their watching faces. "I'm still confused. How did I get here? Why can't I remember—it's so frustrating not to know!"

Dr. Li stayed my temper. "A percentage of amnesia is common in patients with your condition. It can be temporary, and the kind of procedure I performed on you is most conducive to recovery. For now, all you can do to understand everything is listen to us."

I scoffed. "Well, then someone tell me already. Quit beating around the bush!"

Annabelle answered. "About a month ago, I got a very strange letter in the mail. It was from Roger Borough, whom I'd never heard of, but it was signed by you, James Steiner. I knew right away something was terribly wrong with this, even before I read the part about you having only a month to live. It was in the tone of the letter: scary, hopeless. Only now do I understand that you were in the middle of having a nervous breakdown. But I believed you, and to be honest I was lonely myself and wanted a man in my life. I always felt I loved you, since we were kids. So I sent you a train ticket and told you to come. After that..." she lowered her head, "things got out of hand. I needed help. First I hired Norma, but that proved ineffective. Eventually you turned up with Dr. Li's business card. So here we sit."

"Let me get this straight, was I really given a month to live? What about the inoperable brain tumor?"

"I'm sorry," Dr. Li said, "but that was a delusion."

I was horrified. "Are you out of your mind, look at me! I look like I was dragged by my ears through a rocky field!"

"Oh you were going to die, there's no question of that. But it was a self-imposed suicide. You weren't confined to the bed. You came and went as you pleased. You were having a nervous breakdown, so you told yourself you had a month to live. You wanted to die and you even gave yourself a time limit; then, you started to focus your will and your *qi* on this task. If you had not come to me when you did, I'm certain you would be dead by now."

"So what about you?" I thrust an accusing finger at Norma. "The hospital sent you?"

"Honey," she said, "Annabelle hired me to look after your crazy ass. I work for a private mental institution—one that would've been more than happy to admit you, but she insisted on keeping you here. I don't know what it is. She must love you or something. All these people must love you. They're here, aren't they?"

I shrank back in the bed. I felt like I would be sick, and then I was, and so I threw up in an empty box beside the bed. When I sat up, they were all watching me but I didn't care. I knew it was true. I knew I had lost my mind.

* * *

Sometime later, Annabelle and I were left alone. Dr. Li gave me a prescription for an herb tonic that he told me to take regularly before Jenny drove him back to the city. My first wife and I said a hasty goodbye; tears welled up in her eyes a little. Beyond that, there wasn't much to say. The years were too many and the pain I thought I'd endured on her part made it so I couldn't be open. She left the way she always tended to leave: without looking back. I imagined she had a husband somewhere waiting for her.

Celeste was still in the house, probably downstairs talking on her smartphone, or perhaps talking to Norma. I thought I could hear her distant voice as Annabelle and I sat in the quiet bedroom.

"It's all so much," I said. I'd managed to get out of bed and into the chair beside her, but my body was aching.

She placed her hand on top of mine and gently pulled it into her lap.

"I think the worst is over," she said. "Now that you've revisited that memory from your childhood, you can start to process it, and then heal. Dr. Li said he'd help you get through this."

I shook my head, overcome with sadness. "I can't believe this is all true. I was *convinced* James and I were two separate people. Christ, it still feels like we are. How can Roger Borough not exist? I thought I was Roger Borough? What does that mean, that I don't exist?"

"You're James Steiner. You have always been James Steiner. Mentally you divided yourself to deal with the pain. Doesn't it say something in the Bible about a house divided?"

"A house divided against itself will fall."

"That's it—which explains your impending death."

It doesn't explain anything, I thought. Only…

"What is it?" she asked. "Why are you frowning?"

"The craziest thing is that deep inside, I actually feel fantastically better. It's just…"

"Yes?"

I lowered my voice. "What about the Time Eater?"

Her eyes widened. She leaned forward, hissing, "Don't mention it ever again. What do we care about some stupid delusion of your Roger Borough self? We will just pretend it never existed."

"But we know it did exist!" I blurted. "We both saw it. Dr. Li even saw it!"

"Dr. Li assured me the Time Eater was just your own personal demons, the side of you split off from yourself, which you projected into the physical world."

"What? Come on. What about those dreams he said he had about fighting an evil spirit, and the book, and everything else!"

She sat up, letting go of my hand. "He did know about the book, and he did battle an evil spirit—but that evil spirit was you!" She jumped up from the chair and hurried out of the room, closing the door behind her. I was alone again. Out in the hallway, I could hear the sound of her sobbing.

* * *

As I lay back in the bed, staring up at the ceiling, mulling things over, Celeste entered the room. She stood by the door for a second, just watching me. I turned slightly to look at her. I remembered her olive complexion and hooking jawline, her rich and curly hair. How many times had I held her face in my hands, how many times had I kissed it, lay beside it, adored it?

Memories crept back in through the crevices of my unconscious; they joined with the other memories that had recently resurfaced, and suddenly I had the full picture and I knew everything that had happened. It flashed before my mental eyes, all the sex and the lies, the fighting and resentment, even her cutting episode. I realized that it had happened to me; I was the one who took her to the hospital the day when the doctors and nurses kept her on suicide watch. This was my life—this whole thing.

I gave an amused grunt. "You been dating anyone recently?"

She blinked at me, then laughed. "Sure, a few flings here and there. Mostly I'm on my own, still get to see my former stepchildren, so that's a nice part of my life. But of course, I cannot have children myself. As you can imagine, I'm still in therapy. I have discovered there's a part of me that hates men and wants to rip their balls off."

For some reason, this made me laugh. I said, "Sounds like it's a good thing I got out when I did."

"Hey, I *let* you out, and don't you forget it."

The air softened as we fell into our old repartee. She came over and sat in the chair beside the bed. When she was closer, I could see a few lines in her face and under her eyes. Those hadn't been there when I was married to her. She had been through a lot.

"I wonder if I can blame you for all this," I said jokingly.

"The hell you can. Blame that man who raped you. He's the one who taught you how to be a rapist yourself. He's the reason you were able to rape me."

"For God's sake, Celeste, how can you say that? The sex was always consensual. I never did it when you didn't want to. I'm not a rapist."

When she didn't reply, the room hung heavily with silence. I decided to change the subject. "Is that who you were talking to on the phone downstairs, your therapist?"

She nodded.

"Is it the same guy we saw for our marriage counseling? Dr...."

"No, it's a new one. Her name's Mary Swede. She's very good. I can give you her number, if you like."

"No thanks. I think I'll stick with Dr. Li."

She shrugged. "Suit yourself. So what are you going to do now?"

My eyes had strayed to the window. Through the opening, I saw the treetops and roofs of the neighboring houses. I listened for the traffic on the street, heard voices, and the sound of a mass transit bus pulling away. I felt totally lost.

"Actually, I have no idea what to do next," I said. "I thought I was one person, and now I am suddenly another. Well, it's more like I thought I was one person who had a friend. It turns out that friend was just my alter ego." I chuckled. "I guess I should be glad. I'm getting two lives for the price of one."

"That's one way of looking at it. And what about Annabelle?"

The thought of her brought a smile to my face. "I think I'm in love with her. I just hope I can keep it together long enough and not drive her away."

"I know how you feel. At this point that's basically the attitude I have to take whenever I get to know someone—which, in my case, never lasts for too long. Hopefully you'll have better luck."

She surprised me by getting up suddenly and climbing onto the bed. I recoiled, not because I was repulsed by her (honestly, I felt drawn to her), but because the idea of sex right now scared the shit out of me.

She sat on her knees and gently hiked up the brown one-piece dress she wore, exposing her bare thighs. With her other hand, she reached up to hold her left breast.

"Come on, what do you say?" she said. "How 'bout once more, for old times' sake? Don't you remember how we used to fuck like bunnies? *Please*, I want you inside me, I want you deep in my soul—"

She fell forward into me, locking her lips around mine, tongue darting out like a savage eel. I returned the kiss at first, overcome by the suddenness, but when she reached down to pull off my shorts, I stopped her, pushed her back.

"No," I said. "I don't want to do this."

Her gaze sharpened. "What are you talking about, of course you do. Are you not a man? Are not all men stupid?"

Her pupils blazed an intense color, hazel mixed with green, and I was reminded of the robot Dr. Stetson had said she could turn on, that part of her that could function by blocking out all her hurt feelings and emotions. I saw her mental illness dancing behind her eyes, the person who wanted to die, die, and die again. I imagined I was seeing her Roger Borough, and that terrified me. I shoved her away, sending her back onto the floor.

Immediately she jumped to her feet, indignant, and said harshly, "Well, it looks like you're just the silly little faggot I always knew you were. Have fun fucking that black-haired freak. That is, if you're able to fuck her."

She snatched her Gucci handbag from the chair and stormed out of the room, slamming the door. I listened to her angry footsteps on the stairs. Only when they sounded far away did I allow myself to breathe.

* * *

A number of days passed. I lay in bed, recuperating, Annabelle attending my needs. Dr. Li returned to perform another acupuncture treatment. He said I was healing nicely and promised to make the trip out once a week to see me—at least until I was well enough to go see him. He gave Annabelle a copious supply of herbs for me to take, wrote her a bill, and went on his way.

We spent a lot of time talking, Annabelle and I. With her help, I was able to form some kind of coherent picture of my past. However, it was far from perfect. My life, I had realized, was like a photograph viewed through a broken glass frame. The lines and shards and cracks distorted the image, so that really there was nothing to see. Only fragments.

But we loved each other; of this there was no question. Despite my obviously "fragile" condition, she had decided to date me and let me live with her in Brooklyn. She offered to help me out of my apartment lease and she even paid someone to move in my things. She was so nice and understanding. I felt I was in danger of being happy.

After a week I was up and walking around, but I got exhausted easily. Part of it, I knew, was the trauma I had undergone while lying reclined in that bed. It was like I had put my muscles through a weightlifting marathon. But part of it was also re-acclimation; I was like a child who had reached the age of toddler.

Annabelle put up with my tantrums, fed me, prepared my herbal tonics, bathed me, and talked with me into the night. We hadn't done much more than kiss since I *broke on through to the other side,* as Jim Morrison would say. I wasn't sure if I ever wanted to have sex again. My final encounter with Celeste had put a bad taste in my mouth, and I still wasn't sure what to make of it. But even with this, Annabelle seemed to be all right.

We never talked about the Time Eater. Not once. Instead, we avoided the subject, and it began to fade into the background of lives. But I thought of it. Oh, how I did. Every night as the sun went down and the night performed its gradual darkening of the window and the room, I thought about it. Sometimes I would get out of bed and throw open the curtains and stare up at the night sky. The stars, the ever changing moon. And I'd remind myself, *those ones over there, the non-twinkling ones, those aren't stars; those are planets...*

But by and large, life was good. We had finally started to move on. No longer did we remain frozen in the past. Time, it seemed, had managed to catch up with us. The way it always does.

Epilogue

Annabelle came through the door, carrying a tray with my dinner and my herbal tonic. She set it on my lap, then took the seat beside the bed. I thanked her and started to eat the steak and peas she had prepared.

"Delicious," I said. "But what about you?"

She patted her stomach. "Ate mine, thanks. You go ahead and enjoy." She watched me intently, her mystical blue eyes burning me down; her long black hair was tied in a ponytail and hung limply over one shoulder. She looked gorgeous.

"What is it?" I said. "Do I have egg on my face?"

She chuckled. "I was just thinking."

"Uh-oh. Any subject I know?"

"Yes, actually, you know this subject well. You're it."

"I'm a bit sick of thinking about myself."

"Did you know it's been six months since you arrived here?"

"It has?"

She nodded. "I remember when I picked you up at the terminal. I couldn't believe how handsome you were."

"I thought you were beautiful," I said, forking steak into my mouth.

We sat quietly while I finished my meal and then downed my tonic. Annabelle took the dinner tray from me and set it on the floor. Then she said, "I need to talk to you about something."

As soon as she spoke the words, I felt it, the old familiar dread, that sense of unease. I couldn't imagine what she might need to talk about.

"Yes. What is it?"

She reached into her corduroy coat and withdrew a folded red cloth. Slowly, she undid the folds, revealing what lay hidden inside. I nearly passed out.

The book—the one I'd used to summon the Time Eater back at Ohio State; the one Dr. Li and his master had found in the mountains around his village—*that book* lay resting on the cloth. It looked, for all intents and purposes, like the most evil thing in the world.

"Where the fuck did you get that?" I asked.

"I found it," she said. "It was underneath the bed mixed in with some of your clothes and things. I noticed it while I was cleaning."

"Well, what should we do with it?"

She shrugged. "I have no clue. I was hoping you'd have some idea."

"Burn it," I said.

But then I began to wonder. *What if this book proves Roger Borough really did exist? If the book is here, a part of this reality, what's to say all the rest isn't real—the Time Eater, James (me), Roger (me)?*

My excitement bloomed. "Give it here, let me take a look at it."

She hesitated, then extended it to me, but before handing it over she gave me a look that said, *You'd better not fuck with me, pal.*

Once I had it in my hands, my whole body thrummed with some inner power. I opened the binding, flipped through the pages, remembering snatches of text. The more I remembered, the more it all started coming back to me, and I felt like a man waking from a very strange dream.

Outside, the sky turned from purple to black. The room became so dark that only the book shone, seeming to glow with supernatural light. A strong breeze picked up, ruffling the pages.

"James?" Annabelle said, her voice filled with terror. "James, what is this? I don't like it. Give me back the book."

She leaned forward reaching out with her hands, but I struck her in the face with the edge of my palm, sending her to the ground. She cried out and tumbled to the darkness below the bed. I felt myself carried upward, toward the ceiling.

"Quit your crying," I said, and suddenly, filled with the most insane feeling of maniacal joy, I laughed. "Me and Roger got a lot of work ahead of us, so you can just fuck off!"

I started to read. My voice filled the room, strange Latin phrases and guttural sounds, words I couldn't even comprehend, let alone pronounce.

"No, James, stop!" came from the floor, but I ignored it. Instead I lost myself in the text, and I closed my eyes, and deep in the darkness of my mind I could see all the stars and planets of the universe being sucked out of existence. I watched the hazy purple form, the giant blotch of darkness, glide silently across my field of vision. It drew everything into its vast, black depths—time, matter, reality—devouring all…

…and I began to grin, like a child, like a happy crazy child…

…reveling in the thought of the world cracking apart.

About the Author

AARON J. FRENCH (a.k.a. A. J. French) is currently a book editor for JournalStone Publishing and the Editor-in-Chief for *Dark Discoveries* magazine—a professional, internationally distributed print magazine specializing in dark fiction, currently on its tenth year of continuous publication and distribution. He has worked with and edited such authors as David Liss, Norman Partridge, Gary A. Braunbeck, Thomas Ligotti, Steve Rasnic Tem, Jonathan Maberry, F. Paul Wilson, Glen Hirshberg, John Shirley, and many others. In 2011 he edited *Monk Punk*, an anthology of monk-themed speculative fiction and *The Shadow of the Unknown*, an anthology of Lovecraftian fiction. Aaron has also served as co-editor for *The Lovecraft eZine*.

Aaron's fiction has appeared in publications such as *Dark Discoveries*, *Black Ink Horror*, *Something Wicked*, *After Death...*, *Beware the Dark*, *Chiral Mad*, *The Lovecraft eZine*, and others. In 2013 "The Order," Aaron's occult thriller novella about a Lovecraftian secret society was published in the *Dreaming in Darkness* collection. He is currently an active member of the Horror Writers Association. His collection of mystical fiction, *Aberrations of Reality*, was published in 2014 by Crowded Quarantine Productions. *The Time Eater* is his first novel.

Aaron is currently pursuing a Religious Studies PhD from the University of California, Davis. His nonfiction articles on Thomas

Ligotti, Alejandro Jodorowsky, and Karl Edward Wagner have appeared in *Dark Discoveries* magazine, while his online column "Letters from the Edge," focusing on the occult, spirituality, rogue scholarship, esotericism, and speculative fiction, is featured on the *Nameless Digest* website. His academic papers "Toward Christian Renewal" and "Journeys of the Soul in the Afterlife: Egyptian Books of the Afterlife and Greek Orphic Mysteries" were published in the peer-reviewed journal *The Esoteric Quarterly*. He is currently a member of the ESSWE, the European Society for the Study of Western Esotericism.

The Gods of
H.P. Lovecraft

James A. Moore

Donald Tyson

Christopher Golden

Adam Nevill

Jonathan Maberry

Martha Wells

Seanan McGuire

Brett Talley

Joe Lansdale

Laird Barron

David Liss

Bentley Little

Douglas Wynne

Rachel Caine

Edited by Aaron J. French

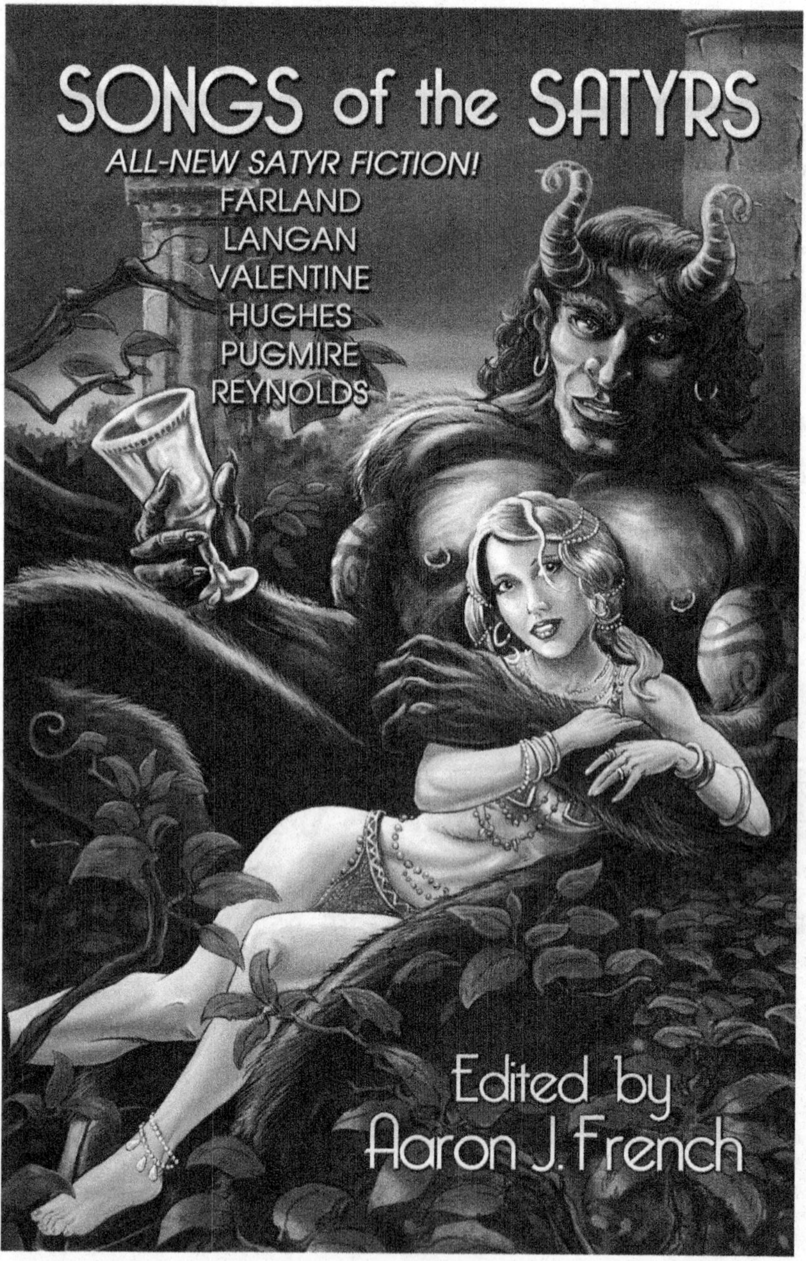
SONGS of the SATYRS
ALL-NEW SATYR FICTION!
FARLAND
LANGAN
VALENTINE
HUGHES
PUGMIRE
REYNOLDS
Edited by
Aaron J. French

CPSIA information can be obtained
at www.ICGtesting.com
Printed in the USA
BVOW09s0521310717
490584BV00001B/7/P